ALONE, BUT NOT LONELY

★ ★ ★

by Tvisha Gupta

YOUNG INKLINGS

This manuscript was published through Society of Young Inklings' Fresh Ink imprint. Fresh Ink is an introductory publishing program for youth writers who have completed a full draft of a novel. This program introduces revision techniques which the youth author then applies to their completed draft. The views of the author are their own and do not reflect the views of Society of Young Inklings.

Chapter Six Poem: *The Black Leaf on the Lilac Tree* by Aadhya Gupta
Cover Illustration: Daria Tavoularis
Interior Design and Layout: Kristen Schwartz
Printed in the USA
First Printing: December 2022
ISBN: 978-1-956380-24-8

To Papa: Thank you for taking me to the library.

CONTENTS

CHAPTER ONE

★ ★ ★

It's a battlefield.

The crowded, student-infested hallways of my private middle school serve as the obstacle course I must overcome in order to make it to the first battle of the school day: Algebra 2 at 8 AM. I'm equipped with no weapons, just weighed down by a heavy backpack that's stuffed with notebooks, folders, and sets of stationery. I take a deep breath and attempt to blink the exhaustion out of my eyes to ready myself to enter the warzone.

Should've called it a night when you finished that Biology lab, Sanah, I groggily think to myself as I trudge through the hallway. *Let this be a lesson to you—never do homework past 11 PM.*

I swerve around groups of chattering, hollering students who have far too much energy for 7:30 AM in the morning. I hastily make way for the large group of athletes running down the hallway as they pass a basketball between them. I step around half-asleep students with cups of still-warm coffee whose lack of consciousness makes them very likely to ruin my sage green cami with an irremovable coffee stain. Exhausted, I finally make it to the large, cemented open area at the center of my school, but groan when I realize the shortcut to my final destination—a long stretch of perfectly cut grass—has turned into a swamp of squishy, wet grass and soil from the bath delivered by the morning sprinklers. I stare down at my pearly white shoes, look back at the grass, then back down.

Not worth it, I think, my whole body slumping. *Just go the long way.*

After an extra, energy-sapping 0.2-mile walk, I finally enter the quad. I can see my destination clearly now: the large, cedar-wood pavilion that stands as the centerpiece of the large expanse. I spot my friends chatting under it and quicken my pace to join them, simultaneously tightening my light green hair clip and adjusting my oversized black jeans as renewed energy flows through me. A couple of people see me approach, and they wave as I walk toward them. One of my closest friends, Fay, jumps up and runs over to me.

"Suns, hi!" she says, tightly squeezing me and latching onto my arm to drag me towards the large table at which everyone is seated. "I like your outfit today. It's so cute. Is this a new hair clip? Ooh, I love your jewelry. You look so pretty. Where is everything from?"

I laugh as Fay continues to pelt me with questions. She's one of the most energetic people I know. She's dressed in a dark red, silk, full-sleeved top paired with a jet black skirt and is wearing a pair of gorgeous chunky black boots. She's pinned her cropped brown hair back with two dark red sage clips and has lined the waterline of her eyes with red eyeliner.

"Hi, Fay," I say, laughing and hugging her back. "I don't remember where anything is from, honestly. I think the top is from H&M? My brain is too tired to remember any details," I finish with a groan.

"Yeah, you look really tired," she says, taking a step back. "Everything okay?"

"I made the bad decision of cramming history notes after 11 PM," I groan, rubbing my eyes. "I feel like I never slept."

"Oh, boy," Fay says, sucking in a breath. "Never work after 11 PM. Life rules."

"Agreed."

"Oy!" I hear a voice cry from my left, and Fay and I turn to look at who cried out.

A smile spreads on my face when I see one of my other friends, Klyah, waving us over. "Fay, my turn to talk to her. Shoo."

Fay and I giggle and scurry over. Fay settles down next to her, and I take a seat on the table, resting my feet in the small gap between my friends.

"Hey, Kly! I like your nails. Super cute." I say, admiring her long, rounded, blue-tipped nails that match her white top, blue skirt, and the book she's reading.

"Thanks, Sun. I got them done yesterday. It's that place that we were talking about the other day, the one near the big marketplace. Super cheap but *such* good quality. We should go someday!"

"Absolutely. Also, you *need* to tell us about that book you're reading when you get a chance. I've been looking for something new to read for a while."

"Oh, gosh, *yes*," she says, sitting up excitedly. "Sit down and let me give you guys the scoop."

I nod my head, quickly greet the rest of my twelve-person group, and then settle in as Klyah shares the plot details of the book she's reading. Fay sits next to me, her head on my shoulder, and we listen intently. The three of us *love* books: it's one of the things we've bonded over the most. Our trio's group chat is filled with constant chatter about plot updates and quotes from our latest reads.

"Hi, gals, what's the chaos about?"

The group instantly quiets down as we recognize the voice, and we all turn to face Silke O'Brien, who walks around the far end of the table and squeezes into her usual spot.

"Anyone wanna spill? Or are we keeping secrets now?" Silke says jokingly, although we all recognize the harsh undertone of her voice.

"Oh, no, of course not," Delhi, Silke's best friend, quickly says, to the rest of our relief. "Some of us were talking about the Mitski concert coming up in a couple of weeks. Do you want to come?"

"Duh. All of you know Mitski because of me. Remember when I brought my speaker to school and played her music for you?" We all nod in sync. "Exactly, so of course, I'm going! All of you can stay over at my house the night before, and then we can get my mom to drive us the next day."

"Sounds fun, thanks, Silke!" Fay says eagerly, and Silke cracks a smile.

Silke tends to be a little … pushy about being open about *everything* we talk about. Nothing wrong with it, though. That's what a friend group is about, right?

The group tentatively returns to its chatty state as we start talking about our weekend plans. Klyah excitedly begins to tell the group about a grand hiking trip she's taking with her parents. It sounds quite quaint— they're traveling to San Luis Obispo and are hitting all the major trails in the morning so they can enjoy the charming town in the evening.

"Oh, Sunny, tell that story about the snake on that hike you did a couple of years ago," Klyah suddenly begs, breaking from the narration of her plans.

The rest of the group exclaims in agreement, and I laugh, shaking my head.

"Kly, I've told this story a million times," I say pointedly, giving her a side stare.

"But it's so funny, please?" she asks. "I'm making my puppy-dog eyes right now. Can you tell?"

"Oh, fine," I say, secretly pleased. It's one of my favorite stories, and it makes me happy to see that my friends care so much. "Alright, so—"

"Wait, Sanah's literally right; we've heard this a million times. Let's talk about something else."

I turn to look at Silke, and she's staring right at me, a bored, uninterested look on her face. The group instantly quiets down, looking between the two of us, their initial interest in my story quickly seeming to dissipate.

"Oh, um, yeah, we can move on," I say haltingly, and she nods, sitting up straight all of a sudden.

"Okay, perfect. Can I share something really exciting? Cool. So, my mom's out of town this weekend, and I get to stay home alone for two days. And that means *total* freedom, and I can go out with whoever I want. Plus ..."

She begins chattering away, and the rest of the girls give her their full attention, turning away from me. I listen in as well, a bit thrown off after

Silke's comment. Silke can be a bit blunt and straightforward sometimes, which doesn't always present itself in the best way. However, she's really nice for the most part, so that trait of hers is something that I usually let go of. We've been friends for a while, and she cares a lot about us: she'll basically do *anything* for her friends. She really took care of me when I first became her friend, and she did the same for every other person in this group. So, we're all happy.

The warning bell cuts into Silke's speech about her newfound freedom, and we all start gathering our stuff to go to class.

"I'll see you guys at lunch," Silke says. "My mom's bringing Chipotle!"

Everyone breaks into smiles at that, and we leave in duos or trios. Fay latches herself onto my right arm and Klyah on my left.

"That's so nice of Silke's mom, bringing us food like that," Klyah says.

"Yeah," I say, agreeing.

I consider bringing up the awkwardness that Silke's comments brought about, but Fay interrupts me before I can.

"Dude, yeah. Silke can be so nice sometimes."

"Oh, um, I know. She's awesome," I say, pushing my thoughts back down. *Another day*, I think to myself. *Or, maybe never. Why start drama? This is just what Silke is like.*

No need to be so sensitive.

My feet thud on the pavement, fast and panicked. My heart is racing, zooming, pounding into my throat. I'm breathing hard, panting as I run even faster, pushing myself to speed up until I begin to see spots in front of my eyes. The only sound breaking the silence around me is the sound of rubber on concrete.

I sprint as fast as I can until a loud beep joins the sound of my feet on the ground, and I slow my pace, doubling over and collapsing on the cold, tundra cement. For a moment, I can't breathe. My stomach is knotted, my lungs have deflated, and breathing in the freezing air ices the insides of my throat and nose. I shut my eyes, allowing my heart to slow, too weak to move a single muscle. Finally, when the lactic acid in my muscles has fermented, and my heart has returned to its normal place, I sit up, squeezing my eyes shut as the world blurs and my head spins. I pull my phone out, terrified to check it, terrified that the near torture I just put my body through didn't pay off. I tap in my password, click on my run-tracker, and with bated breath, check my time.

3 miles in 27 minutes.

A frown spreads across my face. *Shoot.*

Body creaking, I cling onto the metal fence next to me and use it to pull myself up, grimacing when I feel the soreness of my muscles begin to set in. I shake out my legs and arms, trying to melt the ice inside my skin, and begin to walk home. With track tryouts a mere 3 weeks away, I've been pushing myself to run our typical three-mile warmup faster and faster. Most of my group is on the team, and they're able to run it in under 24 minutes, which is what I've been aiming for. I clearly wasn't doing so well with that goal. I need to be captain this year, not just because I've been working hard for it ever since I joined in sixth grade, but because it looks really good on my applications to private high schools, which aren't too far away. However, I force myself to put that concern aside as I look up at the sun dipping below the roofs of the houses across from me. The sky turns darker and darker, dabbed with purple, pink, and yellow, and I breathe in deeply. This is my favorite part of being on track: getting to watch the sunset after my runs each evening. During the season, I have to go to practice after school, and the sun usually sets on my drive home. During the off-season, though, I make it a priority to time my runs according to the twilight, just so I can catch the best part of the evening. However, with this sunset comes the evening California cold, and I start walking to get home and out of the chilly air.

I jump over the cracks in the sidewalk as I walk, turning up the music blasting through my headphones. As I turn into my long street lane, I take in the lights on the roofs of the tall, modern houses. All the families in my neighborhood are very close, and every month, we band together to decorate our houses with a particular theme. For October, we've chosen to adorn our roofs with orange lights, and we spent the entirety of last weekend shifting ladders around and lugging large rolls of lights to completely decorate our tall, patterned roofs. As I turn into my driveway and walk up the slope, ready to get out of the cold, I hear the faint sounds of Bollywood music echoing from the general vicinity of the kitchen. I creak open the door and slip off my shoes, listening to the comforting sound of Indian spices crackling in my mother's pan and breathing in the faint aroma of turmeric and chili.

"MA?" I yell. "I'm home!"

"Hi, *beta*! I'm in the kitchen," she yells back as I walk into the large expanse of overflowing yellow rice and peanuts.

Boxes of puffed rice line the countertops, and *namkeen*, green chili, and chutney are scattered in between. The island in the middle of the kitchen is stuffed with grocery bags, and I start putting them into the cupboards as I continue lightly chatting with my mom.

"So, I'm guessing you're making *poha*," I say jokingly, more than aware that it's exactly what she's making. "I wasn't really sure at first, but I think the seven boxes of puffed rice speak for themselves."

"Very funny, Sanah," my mom grumbles, a small smile on her face. "We're hosting a potluck at work tomorrow, and I'm making the appetizer; thus, the food overflows. Besides, you get this for breakfast tomorrow too, so it's a win-win situation. I have some paneer cooking in the pressure cooker for dinner, so get washed up."

"Delicious," I say, excited, and she grins at that. "I'm going right now. Is dad asleep? I can wake him up."

"No, let him nap. He was exhausted after work today because he got really little sleep last night," my mom says, waving her hand at me.

I nod and attempt to give her a quick hug, to which she exclaims in opposition, complaining about my sweat-stained workout hoodie. I giggle and then run upstairs to take a quick shower, careful not to disturb my dad on the way. I pull on my most comfortable pair of sweats and my favorite light blue hoodie, comb and dry my wet hair, apply some healing serum to my skin, and make my way down the stairs. As I walk back into the kitchen, I sigh when the familiar smell of the spicy Indian curry, *roti*, and *raita* overwhelms me.

"You look extremely comfortable right now," my mom says.

"Just about ready to fall asleep, actually," I say, playfully falling back on one of the kitchen walls and pretending to collapse into slumber.

We both giggle, and I walk forward, stealing one of the roasted peanuts she's kept to cool on a plate and wincing when it burns my tongue.

"Hey! Wait for us to all eat," my mom says, and I yelp when she swats at me with her spatula. "Now go wake your dad before you fill your stomach with snacks and miss out on my delicious food."

"Will do!" I say and run upstairs, taking the steps two at a time.

I walk into my parent's bedroom and switch on a lamp to fill the room with some light. My dad is fast asleep on the bed, but when the light hits him, he turns over a bit. The room is polished from my mom's afternoon cleaning session, and her dresser is perfectly arranged with jewelry and perfume. My dad's laundered clothes are stacked on the large, beige armchair in the right corner of the room, and I giggle, knowing that my mom will soon be lecturing him about not putting them away in time. I walk over to the window and pull open the dark, navy curtains in an attempt to let some of the dimming light from outside in.

"Yeah, I know, I'm getting up," I hear him mumbling, and I giggle, turning towards him.

"Mama made paneer if that's any motivation for you."

My dad groggily opens his eyes and begins to sit up. "That absolutely is. I'll be downstairs in ten minutes."

I smile. My family has the same main trait: food always gets us going.

I leave my dad to get himself out of his sleepy stupor and then skip down the steps to chat with my mom until my dad comes down. When he does, I help carry dishes of hot, steaming, delicious paneer and a hot case of *roti* to the table. When my dad comes down, we all sit around the table and dig in. As I swallow the first mouthful, the spice of the curry fades as its sweet aftertaste settles on my tongue, joined by the wheaty, buttery taste of the *roti*. The tangy *raita* serves as the perfect, cold contrast to the sharp flavors of the main dish, and I sigh contentedly. I inhale my food, starving after the long run I had. My parents and I chatter animatedly all throughout dinner, excited to share our tales from the day. My mom and dad are my best friends, more than any person I've ever met. Naturally, I tell them every detail about my life, and it works the same the other way. Our bond is something that I'm incredibly grateful for, one that I try to strengthen every single day.

After dinner, we begin to clean up the house. My dad cleans the dishes, my mom clears up the dining area, and I get out the vacuum. We blast energetic Bollywood music to keep us entertained as we clean, and when we're all done, we collapse onto the couch.

"Got time to watch a little bit of a movie?" my dad asks, reaching for the TV remote and giving me a hopeful look.

"Yup," I nod, smiling. "Finished most of my homework before my run, and I can finish the English readings in bed. Let's do it!"

As the familiar title music of our favorite Bollywood movie begins to play, I settle back into the comfortable cushions of the couch, allowing myself to be drawn into the thrilling world of the characters.

My phone dings a couple of times while we watch, and when I look at it, it's a text from Silke. She's bugging me for homework answers, which I don't typically give out because I don't want to set a precedent as someone who only does her work for others. However, her texts begin to take on an increasingly annoyed tone the longer I don't respond, and I turn my phone over. It's making me anxious, and I'm too tired to engage.

"Everything okay?" my dad asks, noticing my furrowed brows.

I nod, and he turns away.

Thirty minutes and countless yawns later, my dad shuts off the movie, moving slowly so that my mom, who's fast asleep on his shoulder, doesn't wake up.

"Time for bed?" he says, nodding in the direction of my room.

"Yup," I say, yawning. "Goodnight, Papa."

"Goodnight, *beta*. Don't forget our run tomorrow morning, okay?"

"Got it!"

I trudge up the stairs, exhausted. My eyes feel like they're magnetically attracted to each other, and when I collapse onto my bed, I shut off my lamp, set my phone on silent, and let myself be whisked away into the comforting world of sleep.

CHAPTER TWO

★ ★ ★

The following day, I'm slumped forward on my desk in history, my last class of the day. *Remember not to wake up at 5:45 and run five miles on a school day, Sanah,* I think to myself, regretting the decision I made earlier that day. I'm in desperate need of a nap. However, I've still got this class to get through before that, so I put my wishes for a sweet escape from exhaustion on hold. Luckily, history with Mr. Harfateh is always a blast, and as he stands up in front of the class, I feel some part of my fatigue leak away. Mr. Harfateh's classroom is super interesting: he's really into the old Marvel comics, so he has large, brightly colored posters on all of the bulletin boards in his room. He has Marvel figurines lined up on his desk, and each of our round tables is named after a Marvel character.

"Alright, class!" he says in his chipper, seize-the-day voice.

He walks over and taps the head of another tired student who's taking a quick power nap, and the kid jerks up, eliciting laughter from the rest of the class.

"Sorry, Clove. School ends in an hour, and you can sleep in your comfy bed then. You'd have much sweeter dreams there anyway."

He slaps his hands together and rubs them quickly. "Today's agenda has been posted on Google Classroom as usual. But—" He stops short, and his eyes go wide as he glances all across the room. "We're going to do something that I don't think I've done in ten years of teaching. We. are. going—"

The whole class waits.

"Off the agenda!" he steps forward and does jazz hands.

The class is still. We're all quiet.

"That's it?" someone calls out, and the whole class starts laughing.

Mr. Harfateh steps back sheepishly, rubbing the back of his head with his hand. "Eh, I'm known to be dramatic. Point is, we're going to have a short lecture today, and then I'm going to introduce the final project that has gotten a pretty bad rap around campus, from what I've heard."

We giggle nervously at that. He's not lying—this project is known to be difficult and one of the most strenuous parts of my school's honor society.

"However, I'm here to help guide you. Plus, I've made one change:

you get to work with a partner this time! *Assigned* partner. Yeah, I see you guys eyeing each other," he says, pointing between two students, and we all laugh. "I've posted the partner list online, and you guys can take out your computers to check right now."

The classroom fills with the rustle and unzipping of backpacks, and I pull out my own as well. I log in, navigate to our online classroom, and click on the PDF with the list of names. I scan it, dragging my eyes down until—

"No," I whisper, sitting up straight in my seat, rigid all of a sudden.

I've been partnered with Cruise Bates.

My mind whirls through the defining event of last year's school drama: the big blowup between Cruise and Silke. Cruise and Silke had liked each other early last year, and they were quite close for the first few months of seventh grade. However, Silke had decided that she didn't really want to get involved in a relationship so early, so she had told him very respectfully that she just wanted to stay friends. But Cruise didn't take that in a good way at all. Silke told us that he continued to bombard her with text messages asking her to reconsider, to try it out, that she wouldn't find anyone like him ever again. Creeped out, Silke blocked him on social media, but Cruise just wouldn't let up. He created a fake account to text her from, but when he realized that Silke obviously didn't care, he was livid. He dedicated that fake account to talking about Silke, and he posted things that said he hated Silke for rejecting him and that he would do anything to get her. Silke was incredibly stressed but simultaneously really dedicated in her effort to trying to end the rumors, managing everything on her own. She didn't want to get the administration involved because she said it would cause more problems. She talked to everyone she possibly could, explaining to them that none of this was true and that there were just some issues going on between her and Cruise that were causing this, problems that she'd hoped they could solve off of social media.

When people found out about Cruise's behavior, he became a social pariah. I mean, no one wants to befriend someone who intentionally hurts another person, right? The social media account disappeared after everybody began to avoid Cruise, and Silke said that he didn't take it down because he was trying to be respectful but because he wanted to remove the negative view that other people had of him. However, it didn't work, as opinions about Cruise have remained about the same since then. Everyone in my friend group despises him. He proved himself to be toxic and self-serving, and I've avoided him as much as I possibly could so far. Until now.

How am I supposed to work with the kid that messed with one of my closest friends? I think to myself, my head spinning. *I want nothing to do with him. But now my grade is dependent on him?*

I look at where Cruise sits on the other side of the room. He's wearing a gray hoodie and a pair of jeans with white Nike Air Forces and is lazily scrolling through the list of names. He stops when he gets to the bottom of the list and then sits up straight as well, obviously having seen the pairing. He turns to look at me, and we make eye contact. I force my eyes to become cold and stormy, shooting icicles his way, and he looks away. I slump down into my seat. This is going to be a blast.

After Mr. Harfateh finishes his lecture, he gives us time to go and talk to our partners. I groan inwardly, my body begging me to use the sluggishness that has suddenly filled me as an excuse not to go to Cruise. I stall as long as I can, but when Mr. Harfateh begins to stare pointedly in my direction, I have to force myself to walk over. As I approach, Cruise doesn't make any effort to get up or look my way. Irritation begins to flow through me, but I push it down. *Be nice, Sanah. It's the only way you both are going to get through this project without ripping each other's heads off.*

"Alright, so," I say, jumping straight into business. I don't want to waste any time on small talk. "We have about thirty minutes of class left, so I was thinking that we could work on creating a timeline for each part of the project. We've got a presentation, visual creation, speech, and essay to write and about a month to finish it all. Since the essay is individual, we can take care of that on our own, but let's talk about the presentation because that's the most important part of it. I'll create and share a document with you, and we can start listing our ideas, and based on that, we can come up with a soft deadline for when we want to finish. The visual creation and speech come from the presentation anyway, so we can worry about those later. Does that sound okay?"

He's quiet.

The irritation begins to build.

"Excuse me," I say in a low voice, rapping on the table. "I asked you if that sounded good?"

Cruise nods but keeps his eyes trained on whatever immensely interesting thing lies in his lap. I roll my eyes. I see why Silke found him infuriating.

"Alright, well, I'll share a doc. Make sure you do the work, please."

I walk away without waiting for a response from him—not that I was going to get one anyway. When I get back to my desk, I create and share a document with him and begin listing topics for our project. Cruise's actions aren't surprising, especially considering the background information I have from Silke. She always repeated that he was *annoying*, and I saw that just now. I sigh, slowing my typing. Working with him will be difficult, and it's something that I'm dreading. Silke's tear-stained face, her trembling hands, and the way her voice cracked as she told us about what had happened ripped my heart apart back when Cruise messed with her. I curl my hands into fists, rage building within me. Cruise was *horrible*, and I'm quite scared that he may just do the same thing he did to Silke if I'm not careful. I have to keep him happy to make sure he doesn't pull a similar stunt with me.

I continue working until the bell rings, and when it does, I quickly pack up my stuff and head out the door. Before I leave, I sneak a glance over at Cruise but whip my head back around when I realize he's looking straight at me. Creeped out, I scurry out the door and spot Fay walking toward our group spot.

"Fay!" I call out, and she turns to look at me, breaking into a big smile as she doubles back to walk next to me.

"Hi-hi! How was history?" she asks.

"Horrible. You're never going to believe who I got paired with for the honors project," I say, shaking my head.

"Fill me in, too, please," I hear, turning around to see Klyah grinning at us. We link arms with her, and then I fill them in about what happened. Both Fay and Kly's faces get dark when I mention Cruise's name and fill with contempt when I mention how he acted.

"Sounds like Cruise," Kly says, an undisguised touch of disgust in her voice. "I can't believe you have to deal with that menace. I wouldn't wish that upon anyone."

"Yeah, I'm a little nervous," I say, looking up at the sky. "After what happened with Silke, I'm terrified that any wrong move will cause him to blow up."

Fay squeezes my arm. "Don't fret, Suns. I don't think anything bad is going to happen. Not if he's learned anything from the way he was treated by the school after the first mishap."

"Oh, I hope so," I sigh, shaking my head.

"Does he seem to have changed at all?" Fay asks tentatively. "Has he gotten any warmer, considering the whole school still hates him?"

"Nope. I kept asking him if he heard what I said about the project and tried to get him to contribute a little more, but he just didn't care. He was really disconnected," I say, shaking my head.

"Dang," Fay says, laughing sourly. "I guess you're just going to have to deal with it, although that sucks, and I'm sorry."

"Yeah, I guess I'll just talk to him as little as I can and just stick to what's needed for the project," I say, and the two of them nod. "But let's talk about something other than him. I need to change my mind."

Fay and Klyah start chattering about the Mitski concert they're going to be attending, and since I'm not going and don't really know anything about the artist, I use their spirited conversation to whisk me away from any concerns surrounding Cruise. I guess I'll just need to force the work needed for the project. As for any form of acquaintance, considering his history with my group, it's completely out of the question.

That ship sank a long time ago.

CHAPTER THREE

★ ★ ★

As I walk into history two days later, the music from my favorite playlist, the one that never fails to make me happy, blares through my headphones on full volume. The first part of my day had gone great. My mom had taken me to get a cheese omelet from my favorite breakfast shop in the morning, and I had received A's on tests from two of my classes. As I sit down in my seat, I'm bopping my head to the beat of the song playing in my ear, and I have a big smile on my face. The rest of the seats around me fill up as the clock inches closer and closer to the start time of class. I pull out my laptop, my smile getting bigger as my favorite song starts to play, and I load up our class page. I tap my fingers on my desk in time with the music and get a few weird stares from the people around me, but I could care less at this moment.

"Ms. Patel!" I hear, and I look around to see who called my name, my face reddening when I realize that it is Mr. Harfateh. "Looks to me like your music is definitely entertaining, and I'm glad that you seem happy. However, class is going to start in less than a minute, so let's put the music away." He smiles brightly at me and raises his eyebrows expectantly.

I nod quietly, a little embarrassed, and take my headphones off of my head. Mr. Harfateh walks over to my desk as I'm opening up my backpack to put my headphones in.

"Sorry, Mr. Harfateh, I'll make sure to not have them on when I enter the classroom next time," I say to him, my voice cracking a little due to the humiliation.

"I appreciate that, but I actually came here to ask you to share your playlists. I'm interested to see what tunes make you so happy!" He winks at me and then walks away.

I smile after him. This is why he's my favorite teacher: he shows his students that he cares about more than just academics. As the bell rings, Cruise walks in quickly and sits down in his seat. A trickle of contempt begins to flow through me, one that turns into a stream as I realize that we must work together on the project today.

I hope he's decided to be a bit more productive today, I silently grumble to myself.

A rustling sound startles me out of my thought process, and I look down at my desk to see a stack of worksheets. I glance around me to see what I must do with them and notice that everyone is passing them to the person behind them. I do the same and feel my heart rate pick up when I realize that it's not a worksheet, but a pop quiz.

"For the few of you looking around in confusion, please get started on this quiz immediately. It's about 15 questions and all multiple choice, so it shouldn't be that hard, but you guys only have about ten minutes to finish this, so chop chop!"

Mr. Harfateh starts to do his usual rounds between our desks, and I quickly pull out a pencil and an eraser to get started. As a rule, I study all of the material that my classes cover at home every night, just in case we get thrown a pop quiz like the one we have today. So, when I look at the questions, I'm unfazed because I recognize the topics in all of them. I breeze through the test, and soon, I'm the first one handing my paper in to Mr. Harfateh.

When I walk up, he smiles at me and whispers, "Wait right here; I'm going to grade everyone's tests as they turn them in. I'll give yours back in a second."

I nod and wait patiently as he looks through the test. He brings out his red pen, the one he calls 'the sword of blood and bad grades,' and twirls it in his hands as he looks through my answers. However, the sword has been unsheathed for no reason because I get every answer correct, and Mr. Harfateh's smile gets wider as he returns my quiz, now marked with a big '15/15'.

"Yet another perfect score, Sanah. Good job," he whispers just for me to hear, and I walk away feeling elated.

As I trod back to my desk, I sneak a look at Cruise. He's filling out his paper, leg bouncing on the ground, and doesn't glance up as I pass by him. When I sit back down at my desk, I lazily switch tabs on my computer, type random letters and delete them, and tap my fingers on my desk as I wait for the rest of the class to finish. More and more people walk up to Mr. Harfateh's desk and return, looking more dejected than elated. I follow each of them with my eyes, leaning back in my chair.

As the last student returns to his desk, this one looking especially unhappy, Mr. Harfateh gets up from his desk and walks to the front of the class.

"Well!" he exclaims, clapping his hands together and rubbing them. "Looks like we need some studying. Pop quizzes are pop quizzes for a reason. Hopefully, some of you learned a little bit about your studying skills and overall level of knowledge. For now, let's go ahead and transition to the group projects we started talking about yesterday. Go ahead and get with your partner and continue working!"

Groaning internally, I force myself to get up and make my way over to where Cruise is sitting. I hope he's in a more conversational mood today because we really need to get stuff done. As I approach him, he fixes his glance on the eraser shavings on his desk. I place my computer on the corner of his desk and squat down next to him, navigating to the tab that has our History project.

"Hi," I say tentatively. "Were you able to get any work done on the project so far?"

He quickly shakes his head, not saying a word or looking at me. I try to spark the conversation once more, scrolling down to the page that has the notes I took on the Boston Tea Party and Mercantilist Policies of Britain, the two topics I found most interesting for the project.

"I took some pretty extensive notes last night on these two topics," I say, turning my computer so he can see it. "They're pretty long, so don't feel obligated to read through them all. I definitely wrote way too much," I finish, chuckling.

Still no response. His face is turned towards the same pile of eraser shavings, and he's bouncing his leg rapidly. I feel the familiar tendrils of annoyance shoot their way through my stomach as I stare at him. Would it kill him to at least grunt in acknowledgment?

"Cruise?" I say, a little more than a touch of irritation in my voice. "It would really help if you acknowledged what I was saying."

He murmurs something softly (he speaks!) and turns his head in my direction ever so slightly. Motivated by that little action, I proceed to give him a run-through of the ideas I had for the project, pulling up the example slides I had researched, the template for the poster, and a brief outline of the speech structure I thought we could use. After three minutes of talking, I quiet down and catch my breath, looking at him to see his response and see if he has any ideas.

Nothing.

He's still staring at the stupid desk.

My short temper reaches its max and pushes itself past my stomach, throat, and then mouth.

"Look, I don't know what your deal is, but you need to either spit it out and tell me or keep it to yourself and *start to work with me*," I say, my voice a low but agitated murmur. "This project is important to me, and I take my academics seriously. If you're going to be one of those partners that just doesn't do any work, then tell me now so I can plan ahead doing all the work myself."

Cruise doesn't look up for the first few moments, but when he does, I see fear pooling in his eyes.

"I'm sorry," he says suddenly, his voice trembling ever so slightly. "I'm so sorry."

I immediately force myself to calm down, slightly confused as to why he seems so fearful. Even though I know that everything I said was totally called for, I would hate for him to feel intimidated because that would just put a bigger dent in our ability to work together. I need to make him feel a little better so that it doesn't impact our work.

"Look, I'm sorry for being aggressive with my point," I say in a low voice. "But it really would help if you started responding. This project is super work-heavy, and the two of us really need to work together if we want to get anything done.

Cruise looks up at me, and my heart starts pounding when I realize that my aggression may have just led to the start of an era where Cruise attempts to hurt me, just like he did with Silke. However, with a slight look of surprise on his face, he sits up, blinking some of the fear out of his eyes.

"Yeah, you're right," he says, his voice still trembling but clearer than before. "I'll participate."

I'm a little taken aback. From what I've been told about him, I wasn't expecting him to back off without a fight. Silke's depiction of him had me ready to deal with leaving the class with two or three vicious lies about me spreading through the class like hair lice or having to deal with Mr. Harfateh intervening and conversing with us about proper classroom etiquette because we ended up in a yelling match.

There was none of that.

But even though he may have avoided a fight this time, there's no telling what could happen in the future. I'm still relying on Silke's experiences with him to guide me through our work together, and that means that I need to interact with him as little as I possibly can. Especially if I want to save myself from any major drama.

I force myself out of my thoughts and look back down at Cruise, who is still looking at the desk. This project is too important for me to worry about drama coming in the way, and I need to make sure that I convey the same sentiment to Cruise.

"Look, we obviously aren't on the best terms right now, and that's fine. I don't think either of us really wants to get to know each other on a deeper level. But for the sake of this project, can we just be cordial? I don't want personal stuff to get in the way of a good grade."

Cruise looks up at me, a blank look on his face, and nods.

"Works for me."

An hour later, I return back to my seat to pack up my stuff. After our conversation, Cruise and I were able to make some pretty good progress today. We finally decided on a topic for our project and were able to start researching;

although we weren't engaged in active conversation as we worked, we were able to settle into a semi-comfortable silence and be productive. As the bell rings, I sling my backpack onto my shoulder and start to walk out the door.

"Sanah!" I hear from behind me, and I turn to see Cruise trying to squeeze through the crowd of kids desperate to leave the classroom. When he reaches me, he holds out his phone. "Would you feel comfortable putting your number in? It would be nice to have a way to communicate about the project."

"Oh, uh, sure," I say, hesitantly taking his phone and inputting my number.

I'm not comfortable with him having my number at all—who knows what he could do with it? However, I'm not active on social media, so this really is the best way for us to communicate. Besides, it's solely for the project, so there shouldn't be much of a problem. I can figure out a way to delete it from his phone after. Also, if Silke finds out, I don't think she'd be too concerned with it either if I just clarify that it was for the project. After putting in all my details, out of habit, I tap on the contact photo icon and snap a quick, silly picture of myself. I wince with realization after I've taken it. *Too friendly. Shoot.*

"What was that for?" Cruise asks, obviously confused.

"For your contact picture of me," I say, handing his phone back to him and deciding to just be honest. "It's a pet peeve of mine when people don't have those little pictures of people when making their contacts. What if you have three friends named Sanah? How do you tell them apart?"

He smiles softly at that, and I'm surprised at how much it transforms his face. He looks like he has a little life in him.

"Cool. I like that. Here, I'll do the same for you."

He holds out his hand to get my phone, and I reluctantly place it in his hand, open to the contacts app. I don't like how friendship-reminiscent this action is, but I can't do anything about it. He inputs his information as well, snaps a silly picture with his tongue out, and hands it back to me. "Here you go."

"Thanks," I say, pocketing the phone. "I'll see you around."

I walk out of the classroom before he can catch up with me, melting in with the rest of the students funneling towards their lunch spots in the strong California sun.

"Sanah?"

I turn to see Cruise towering over me and stumble back a bit, startled. *Why is he* following *me?* I'm quite close to the spot where my group usually meets, and if they see me talking to Cruise without any explanation, they would be livid.

"Sorry, but I just wanted to ask if I could text you about the project tonight so we could decide on the next steps?" he says, looking straight at me.

Uncomfortable, I look away and around me to make sure none of my friends are around before responding.

"Yeah, that's fine. You don't need to ask permission for that," I say, bouncing anxiously on the balls of my feet.

"Alright, cool," he says, nodding and stuffing his hands into his pockets. There's a few moments of awkward silence, in which he doesn't budge. *Does he want me to talk to him?* I think. My panic levels slowly begin to rise, and I realize that I *really* need to get out of there.

"Okay, cool, bye."

I practically bolt out of there and just in time, too, because Fay and Klyah come around the corner at the very moment I turn away from Cruise.

"Sunny!" Fay says, waving me over, and I speed over to join them. When the three of us have walked closer to our lunch spot, I turn to look back at where I left Cruise. Even from a distance, I can see that his eyes have become stormy once more. I hold eye contact for just a few milliseconds before turning away and picking up speed. I'm not really sure what he expected me to do just then. Actively engage in conversation? Look happy to be there? He can't just expect me to get over something that hurt one of my friends and demolished his reputation. It was his fault—he has no one else to blame.

My friends and I walk into the seating area and plop down, jumping into a conversation about a *gorgeous* new piece of jewelry that Klyah's parents bought for her—a silver necklace with a white lining and onyx all down the centerline.

"So, Suns," Kly says, looking at me curiously and suddenly changing the topic. "How's it going with Cruise?"

"Yeah, I mean, he's still quiet," I say, and they both roll their eyes. "I'm definitely unsure about how we're going to work together because he seems very aloof."

"Sounds like Cruise," Klyah says, shaking her head. "Silke always said that he would totally check out when he wasn't interested in something. I just hope this doesn't impact your grade as much, though. This project is a major deal, from what I hear. But also, you're so capable of doing this on your own, so if he's being a brat, I don't think you have much to worry about."

I smile at Kly. "Thank you, that's sweet. He did do *some* work today after I called him out for doing nothing, so that's some kind of an improvement, at least."

"I mean, I guess," Fay says. "But, like, he's also a jerk. He just did what he was supposed to for class today. That doesn't mean he's automatically a way better person."

"Oh, for sure," I say, shaking my head. "I think he's just putting on a show for the sake of the project, which is fine with me. It's not like I want to get to know him or anything. Anyways, let's change the topic. Did you guys see that the library got a new stock of YA books?"

The two of them nod at that, and we let the topic of Cruise fade away as the rest of the group begins to join us around the table. As excited chatter surrounds us, I let myself think about Cruise once more. If we can keep up the formality we have right now, I think we can make it through the project without too many issues. However, I need to make sure that the friendliness he showed towards me afterward isn't reciprocated at all, just so that he doesn't fall under the wrong impression that I'm interested in being friends because I'm not. At all.

I just need to get this project done. Then, I can let go of Cruise for good.

CHAPTER FOUR

★ ★ ★

Later that day, I'm sitting on a worn-out, light blue bean bag in my room with a blanket draped over me and my laptop on my thighs, working on a short story for a competition that I'm interested in entering. I finished a three-mile run right after I got back from school, and since writing after being freshly showered is one of my favorite feelings, I've been seated on my beanbag for nearly two hours as I type away. Creative writing has always served as an outlet for me. Channeling my muddled, raging emotions about discomforting experiences into the actions and feelings of my characters gives me much-needed distance from any experienced issues. As those characters wrangle with problems similar to my own, I write out a positive sequence of events for my characters to gain reassurance that things in my own life will eventually settle down, regardless of how tumultuous they seem. Lately, I've been feeling pretty frustrated with my running times, so I decided to write a thriller story to be able to channel my frustration into the struggles of the main character as they attempt to escape their dangerous surroundings. To curate the perfect writing environment in my room, I've switched on all my lamps and fairy lights so the room has a soft, yellow glow. Outside, the sun is setting, the sky a canvas of pink, purple, blue, and yellow watercolors. I've connected my phone to my room's speaker to play soft jazz music in the background. A quiet clicking noise from my keyboard fills the room, and as I sink into my writing, the ideas begin to flow faster and faster. I block out everything around me, and the dark, treacherous environment I've created in my writing begins to surround me.

A knock on my door takes me out of the world I've created, and I look up to see my mom pop her head through the door.

"Hi, *beta*. Are you free to talk for a bit? I just got back from some errands, and I didn't get to see you after school," she says. Upon noticing my laptop open, she quickly adds, "Oh, if you are working, then we can chat before dinner."

"No, no, I was just finishing up," I say, and close my laptop.

I put it aside and scoot over, making space for my mom to sit. My mom comes and sits next to me, and we both go under my blanket, getting cozy for our usual evening chat.

"Ok, so you go first, and then I'll go," she says.

I nod my head and begin to tell her about my day. This is how we usually talk—I'll tell her every little detail about my day, and then she will do the exact same. There's a lot to tell her about today, and I especially want to talk to her about the situation I had with Cruise and my moral dilemma.

My mom listens closely to what I have to say as I describe in detail the encounter I had with Cruise. Her eyebrows raise when I tell her about the things I said and the way Cruise reacted, but she cracks a smile when I tell her about the way I apologized to him and about our information exchange. When I'm done talking, I take a deep breath.

"Alright, I'm done. I can tell that you have a *ton* to say just by the look on your face, so I'll let you talk."

She laughs at that. "Well, firstly, I'm glad that you were able to tone down your response to Cruise. Being mean is never the way to get what you need from someone."

I nod when she says this. Even though Cruise has clear issues, being rude to him is going to lead us nowhere.

"However, I'm noticing a *ton* of hostility on your part. I do want you to consider observing him a little more to see if he's changed," she continues. "While I'm not saying that what he did to Silke is alright at all, it's been a while since that event. He may just have changed his behavior since then. Since you're friends with Silke, it does make sense to me why he would be a little closed-off and match the things you've been told about him by Silke: he obviously has history with you guys, so your interactions are bound to be stilted. However, everyone deserves a second chance, especially if they've been given the time to learn from their mistakes. You'll never know if someone has made a change unless you give them a chance to show it."

"But Cruise's actions put Silke in the worst mental state during the fiasco," I protest, feeling slightly defensive of Silke. "Can someone really make such a big personality change?"

"You'd be surprised how much people can change, especially if they've gone through something that completely changes the way they live their life," my mom says, smiling softly. "When you lose relationships, lose respect, or lose social standing, that's more than enough motivation for someone to realize that they need to make a change. I understand your loyalty to your friends: it's admirable. However, I'm requesting you to keep your friendship with Silke separate from your project with Cruise and take a look at his personality from your *own* eyes, just so that he can be given a second chance that I think all people deserve."

I take in what my mom is saying, turning it over slowly in my mind. I understand my mom's philosophy in theory, but I don't think it's applicable to this situation. I don't think that *everyone* deserves a second chance, especially if their actions have deeply hurt someone. Cruise hurt Silke, one of my closest friends, which completely justifies my wariness. I'm also worried about opening up to him and then going through something similar to what Silke did. What if he totally flips out because he hates that I say no to an idea of his? He's already proven that he doesn't like rejection. If he starts pulling the same stuff he did with Silke because I let him show more of his personality, I wouldn't be able to get over it. Plus, Silke would *murder* me if she ever knew that Cruise and I were friends in any way.

There are some people that don't deserve a second chance.

Cruise is one of them.

About an hour later, my mom gets up to exit my room. I stretch my muscles, a little stiff from sitting down for so long, and then lean over to grab my laptop to do some research for the project. Right before my mom exists, she turns back to look at me.

"I wanted to ask why you didn't go to dinner with your friends today?" she asks.

Bewildered, I stare at her.

She continues and says, "I saw your friends at that little French restaurant near the grocery complex. You should have gone with them. You've been working so hard lately; it would have been a nice chance for you to take a break. Tell us when they go out next, we'll drive you."

There's a huge lump in my throat, and I can't swallow it, so I just nod at my mom. She nods back and exits my room, shutting my door silently. I stare at the door for a few moments, thinking about what she said. *So they went out to dinner without me,* I think. There's a sinking feeling in my stomach and I feel … I don't know how I feel. I do know that the group does do stuff in duos or trios frequently. But I'm confused about why they wouldn't invite me if it was something that the whole group did. It would have been nice to get a quick text from Fay or Klyah.

I grab my phone and look through my messages to see if I missed some information about this, but there's nothing there. I let my hand drop with my phone in it and take a deep breath, letting it out with a sigh. *Get over it, Sanah,* I think. *It is what it is.* I stare back down at my phone again and, even though it's stupid and futile, wait for a message from the girls.

When I get a message notification a few seconds later, I'm beyond surprised. *Wasn't expecting that manifestation to work that well,* I think. When I open the messages app, though, the initially sad feeling I had converts to one of complete surprise, as the notification is from … Cruise?

Hey

hey

hope your evening is going well

oh, thanks. hope urs is good too
did u need something?

just wanted to make sure that i had the right number. this
is sanah, right?

yes, it is.

cool. i also wanted to let you know that i managed to bag
us an interview with a Stanford history professor for the
project.

woah, hold on. really?

yup. emailed just about everyone i could find on their
website who had the smallest affiliation with the history
department and i managed to get one. it's scheduled for
this weekend on a video call.

holy crap, that's incredible
that's going to be a really awesome addition. thanks.

definitely. since this is a group project, i was wondering
if you would be interested in coming over to my house
so that we could both be present in the interview? i think
we'd both be able to ask good sets of questions to get the
most information out of him.

I pause at that. Go over to his house? I'm not sure how much Silke would like that. Plus, that sounds more like something that close friends would do. We are *nowhere* near that.

> is there any way we could do it at school?

> i asked him about potential interview times, and unfortunately, he's only free at times in the evening. my dad also has a really high-tech video call set up, so that could make any video recordings we make of the interview for our slides come out with far better quality.

I sigh. He's got a point. This project needs to have everything be *perfect*, especially since past iterations that haven't reached that level haven't scored as well. As someone who plans to apply to private high schools, getting a good grade on this is of the utmost importance because not only does it mean I solidify an A in history, but I could get Mr. Harfateh to write a recommendation letter for me. I need to do well. Every aspect of this needs to be perfect. I sigh and type out a message to him.

> alright. send me the details and ill be there.

> cool. see you then.

I don't bother responding to the last message and put my phone down next to me. While I'm not really happy about having to go over to his house, getting a Stanford professor to provide us with information is a really great addition to our project. But what's most surprising is that *Cruise* bagged this interview. From the way Silke has portrayed him, he would be the last person to put so much effort into such an endeavor. My mom's words from before creep into my mind, and I feel a few tendrils of doubt about Cruise's character begin to rise up to the surface. Maybe he really has changed?

No, Sanah.

I pound the tendrils back into the ground, burying them deep under the surface so they can't see the light of day. He still did mess with Silke, and while he seems to be sort of dedicated, I can't trust him yet. Cruise is still on my warning radar, and he's going to have to do a little more to get off of it.

CHAPTER FIVE

★ ★ ★

The next day, when I get to class, instead of waiting around for Mr. Harfateh to tell us to get with our group, I walk over to Cruise's desk right away. Even though we're on very shaky terms, I want to thank him for getting us that interview once more because it really is a great feat.

As I approach, Cruise looks up from his phone at me, his face turning stony. However, I shoot him a small smile to let him know that I come with peace, and the stone seems to crack a bit.

"Hey," he says tentatively, and when I nod at him, he straightens up.

"I wanted to thank you for setting up that interview once more," I say a little hesitantly.

It's the first time I've been willingly nice to him, and it feels a little awkward.

However, he smiles when I say that, his eyes a little brighter than they were when I first approached. "Of course. Anything for the project, right?"

"Absolutely."

Mr. Harfateh begins to talk at that moment, and we both turn to look at him. However, I don't feel the need to return to my desk to get as far away from Cruise as I possibly can: being in his general vicinity seems … tolerable for now.

"Nothing much to say today, folks," Mr. Harfateh says. "Go ahead and get straight to work. I'm here if you need help."

The classroom begins to bustle, and I start to head back to my desk to grab my laptop.

"Do you want to work outside?"

I turn around to see Cruise staring straight at me, clearly nervous about my response. I take a quick look through the windows to check the weather, perking up when I see how sunny it is. I don't *really* want to work alone with him, but campus is really quiet during class, and working outside in the sun could be really enjoyable. We'd also be able to talk through the interview questions we need to write today in a more peaceful setting because the classroom is getting noisier by the minute.

"Sure," I say, deciding to stop overthinking the decision. "Let me grab my computer, and we can sit on a lunch table outside."

His face momentarily takes on a look of immense surprise. It clears up the very next second, but we both know that I saw it. I turn around and walk back to my desk to avoid any awkwardness, but I understand his surprise: people in my group aren't supposed to like him. And I don't. I just want to work in a nice atmosphere. It just *happens* to be with him.

We grab our stuff and head outside to work in the sun, taking a seat on some of the red lunch tables right outside the classroom and getting right to work. Although I'm initially nervous that people from my group may see us, there seems to be no one outside, so I relax. We settle into a surprisingly comfortable silence, the sound of our clicking keyboards filling up the bubble of focus around us. Towards the end of the period, we have a long list of questions for our interview.

"Wow," I say, stretching my arms up above my head. "We're way ahead of schedule."

"Right? Good job to us," Cruise says, and despite us both clearly not wanting to, we smile.

We pack up our stuff and head back inside, waiting for the bell to ring. Wordlessly, we walk out next to each other, slowly making our way through the crowded hallways, swerving around large groups of friends, and moving ourselves into the soft sun peeking through the gray sky. As we approach the main hallway, close to where my friends sit, I feel the same dread about them thinking too much of our nonexistent friendship. However, it feels wrong to just walk away. We aren't complete strangers anymore, so I turn to say goodbye more definitively.

"Text me the details about Saturday, okay?" I say, bringing us to a stop.

"Sounds good," he says, nodding. "Good work today."

"You too. That Stanford professor better appreciate the hard work we put into this."

"He will. Besides, we can just cut him out if he doesn't. So what if he's a Stanford professor? *We* hold the power here," he says, grinning.

I let out a laugh. "Bye, Cruise."

"Bye, Sanah."

We turn away from each other, and I begin to walk to my group's spot when I'm stopped by a voice that sends chills down my spine.

"Was that Cruise?"

My heart sinks as I recognize the voices behind me. I turn to see Fay and Kly looking straight at me, a confused look on both their faces.

Shoot, I think to myself.

"Um, yeah," I say nervously.

They stare straight at me, a cold, dirty look on their faces. They seem to be getting more suspicious by the second, and I know that I need to fix this right away.

"I was just talking to him about one part of our project," I say a little hesitantly, rubbing the back of my neck with my hand.

"I mean, with the amount of time you guys were talking for, I think you were talking to him about more than just the project," Kly says, folding her arms and furrowing her brows.

"He tends to overshare," I say, quickly trying to cover up. "In order to keep myself in his good graces for the project, I'm trying to pretend like I genuinely like interacting with him. Besides, he's got connections to some really great sources, and I want him to want to get them for the project. That can only happen if he feels like he has a good working environment, and I'm trying to curate that for him."

"Cruise and work on a project? That sounds really unlike him," Fay prods, narrowing her eyes.

Swallowing ever so slightly, I respond, "Yeah, I whisper-yelled at him a few days ago to get his act together and start contributing. As much as I know that I can do this on my own, I'd prefer that he doesn't take credit for something that was obviously a spectacular demonstration of my own work."

Their faces clear up at that. "Good work," Kly says. "He definitely needs someone to yell at him. He probably never had someone teach him right from wrong when he was growing up, and it's pretty apparent."

They walk forward and link arms with me, dragging me to our lunch spot while chattering away about class. I pretend to listen and try to ignore the small trickle of guilt about lying making its way through my stomach.

It's just a small lie, I think. *You still don't know what he's really like. No point feeling guilty. No need to be nice to Cruise when staying loyal to my friends is what really matters.*

Later that evening, back at home, I'm curled up in my parent's bed, under their 4-layer, light blue, incredibly soft, and comfortable quilt, working on a private high school application. The soft taps on my trackpad and the occasional typing frenzy when I get a spark of genius for an essay are the only sounds that fill the room. I hear a tap on the door and call for the knocker to come in. My mom creaks the door open, and I immediately smile when I see her.

"Hi *beta*, free to talk?"

"Yes, please," I say, eagerly shutting my laptop and lightly tossing it aside. My mom slides in next to me, pulling the covers over her.

"May I ask why you're in our bed?" she questions, an amused look on her face.

"Because your quilt is the single most comfortable thing I've ever felt. I would take this for my own room if it wasn't twice the size of my bed."

My mom laughs, a tinkling, comforting sound. "Ah, yes, so sorry for buying a quilt that was the size of our bed."

We both giggle, and then I begin telling her about my day. When I get to the part about the small lie I told Fay and Kly, she frowns a little.

"Hmm, I'm not sure if I agree with that," she says, looking at me.

"Really?" I ask. "It was just a small one to clear up some confusion that my friends had. How does it matter?"

"Even though a white lie seems harmless when you tell it, it always becomes something more," my mom says. "One lie always leads to another, and before you know it, you're going to have fabricated an entire story that isn't true. I know that Cruise is perceived as a terrible figure by your group. He may even be one. But keep this in mind: lies, big or small, always add up."

"Good point," I say, genuinely meaning it.

She's right: lies always tend to come back in the worst way. However, a tinge of doubt remains in my mind. If narrating these lies keeps me out of trouble with my group and even puts me in their favor, especially since there's *some* truth to them, then as long as I can keep them from getting out, I'm sure that no harm can be done. Right?

"Mama, quick question," I say, trying to understand her perspective better. "I know you've mentioned the importance of being impartial going into this acquaintance with Cruise, but look, realistically, Silke did go through a lot. I've had a bit of doubt about him because of what I heard about him from my friends, and I'm not sure how to stop that from impacting my perception of him."

She lets out a *hmm*, and sits back, leaning on the headrest. "I get your mindset. Loyalty is definitely important, and it's admirable that you're so loyal to your friends. However, you need to remember that you are separate from them. Your loyalty can impact your behavior toward a person, but I don't think it should impact your *opinion* of them: that should be based on your own perception. This doesn't mean I'm asking you to not be cautious. As a female, hanging around any boy that has a history of being inconsiderate of women is a little anxiety-inducing, so you should definitely keep your guard up. However, don't let the words of other people overwhelm you. You can be cautious and observant at the same time."

I let my mom's words sink in. She's right. I've definitely changed my own interactions with Cruise and narrowed my perceptions of him because of my loyalty to my friends. I did it just a few hours ago. But … it's *Cruise*.

"By blurring your perception of Cruise based on what your friends say, you're going to be solely focused on the bad parts of his personality, and that's unfair to him. Be cautious, but give him a chance to be who he truly is. See what you think of him then," my mom says.

My mom gets up quickly after that to shut off the pressure cooker, apologizing as she exits the room, but I use the alone time to think about what she said. I don't think my mom understands that if I even attempt to open up my mind to Cruise, I'll lose every other friend I have. Just the thought of that sends chills down my body, and I shake my head, attempting to get rid of the anxious feeling that has settled in my stomach. While giving him a chance is the moral thing to do, I'm not sure if it's worth the risk.

My mom pops her head in a few moments later to tell me that dinner is ready, and I painstakingly untangle myself from my soft, comfortable heaven. However, I fall back into the pillowy covers when I hear the ding of a text message as I lean over to grab my phone. My eyes widen a little when I see a text from Cruise. *Wow, that's freakishly perfect timing.*

Hey, just wanted to confirm that you were still coming over tomorrow, right?

I hesitate for a second. One part of me still isn't sure what his intentions are, and I still feel myself returning to my original, naturally loyal self. I trust Silke wholeheartedly, and I don't want to disregard what she says. Despite my mom's words echoing through my mind, I'm not sure that taking the risk of losing my friends is a good idea. However, I need that recommendation letter. I need that A. If I have to see him for that, then so be it.

I take a deep breath and type out my response.

yup. see you soon

CHAPTER SIX

★   ★   ★

The first thing I notice about Cruise's house is that it's *stunning.* The garden in front of his porch is full of multicolored flowers, and small, star lights hang from the roof. The front lawn is just starting to grow, but signs of support for the LGBTQ+ community, the Black Lives Matter movement, the #MeToo movement, and a variety of other social justice movements cleanly line the borders of the grass. The house is painted a dark, elegant shade of navy blue, finished with white on the rims. The window shutters are white as well, all wide open and lined up symmetrically with each other. My mouth is wide open as I walk up the stone path to his front door, and drops a little wider when I see the state-of-the-art security system doorbell that I get to press.

Within a few moments, I hear footsteps coming down the stairs from inside.

Remember, Sanah, I tell myself. *Do whatever you gotta do for that A.*

The door unlocks, and there stands Cruise in a pair of dark blue sweats, a light pink sweatshirt, and … hot pink bunny slippers?

"Nice slides," I point out, snickering.

He looks downwards and is immediately embarrassed.

"Oh, they're my mom's; I just couldn't find my own," he says, frantically kicking off the slippers. He pushes them under a white, padded bench to get them out of sight. "You know, my normal, black, store-bought slippers."

"Oh, yes, your normal black slippers. Although I must say, the hot pink bunny slippers are real eye-catchers. Really brings the girls in."

"Shut up."

I let out a chuckle, and he cracks a grin too. It's a different look on him. It transforms his entire face completely.

"Let me grab some snacks, and we can go sit in the living room," he says before walking towards the kitchen.

As I wait for him to return, I find myself gravitating toward the big wall in the entrance hallway. It's covered with frames that contain cut-out pieces of newspaper joined together to form beautiful quotes or poems. I recognize some popular limericks and haikus, but there are a few that I have never seen before, likely written by Cruise's family. I walk down the hallway towards the main door to read all the pieces of writing, and I don't notice Cruise coming up behind me.

"Leaving already?" I hear, and I start a little.

I whip my head around to see him and see a plate of sandwiches and a bowl of goldfish in his hands. He looks a little bewildered, and I understand what he was thinking.

"Oh, gosh, no, I'm not leaving. I was just looking at the wall," I say hastily, gesturing to the wall.

"Ah, yes, what my mom likes to call the 'wall of words.'" He starts walking away from me, smiling as he looks at the different frames on the wall. "My family has had this ever since I was little, and we are always adding to it. My mom was an English major before she went to law school, and my dad minored in English before business school, so they both love writing. I'm always trying to come up with pieces of writing that are good enough for this wall because my mom is pretty selective about what goes on here."

He's a writer? *Him?* I think, a little astonished. I would never have taken Cruise to be the type to write.

"Is any of your writing on here?" I ask him, curious to see something he's written.

He shakes his head at me. "Not yet. As I mentioned, my parents are pretty selective with what goes on here, so the only things that are here are pieces from them and my siblings. But I think the piece I'm currently working on has some potential. It's missing *something*, but I can't really understand what it is. I'll figure it out, though."

"Can I see some of your work?"

He turns to look at me, surprised that I seem to care. I'm surprised that I care, too. I'm curious about this new hobby of his and want to know more.

"Really?" he asks.

"Yeah, if you're comfortable. I'm a writer too, and I know how difficult it is for me to share my work with other people."

"No, I'd be happy to," he says, smiling. "Let me go grab some of my work."

He scurries out of the room, and I hear his footsteps as he walks upstairs. I turn back to the wall, examining it further. His mom's pieces are especially gorgeous. She doesn't use the typical structural convention for her creative writing pieces but puts an artistic writing twist on them to help evoke emotion.

"Here," I hear from behind me, and I turn to see Cruise walking towards me with a folder of some of his work. He reaches out to hand it to me. "Here are some of my best pieces. Granted, there's still some work to be done, but I really like these ones."

I take the folder from him, flip it open, and begin to read. He mostly writes poetry, and I'm guessing that his mom's standards are quite high because these poems are beautiful. There's one in particular, though, that catches my eye.

From a thousand miles away, I can hear the black leaf, lightly detaching itself from the towering, vivid purple lilac tree,

It flutters slowly, swirling around in circles around three times before it pats the ground,

It stretches as it sinks into the puddle of the fresh, raw rainwater,

As light streams of water form beside the slanting road curb, it goes down the water slide doing loop-de-loops on the way down,

It smacks the dead end and gently unwinds, the brisk breeze grabs onto its stem and carries it on its back,

It soars like a plane and spins all around, higher, higher, the breeze does go,

It can see Earth, Venus, Jupiter and Mars, until the breeze lets go and the leaf is all alone,

Falling, falling back down to earth, It closes its eyes as it feels himself letting go of all the memories and haunting imagery,

Bit by bit, its roots start to separate, parting from the rest of its body, ripping, ripping, as the stem releases its piercing grasp and breaks its promise of never letting go.

Splitting, splitting, into a million pieces as it clunks right into the abyss.

"Woah," I say, closing the folder and handing it back to him. "These are really, really well-written, especially the one with the leaf imagery. Your mom has super high standards because I think they're super worthy of being on this wall."

"Thank you," he says, taking the folder back and smiling. "My brother always says that as well, but I think my mom does it to push me to improve even more. Even though it can get difficult at times, I appreciate that she does it. It motivates me to work harder."

"Positive way of thinking. You mentioned more than one sibling, right?"

"Yup, I've got a sister too. They're a lot older than me, though. My brother is at Yale for law school currently, and my sister just graduated high school last year. She's at UCLA for Economics."

"Oh, so each sibling is following in the footsteps of one of the parents, I see."

"Yeah, pretty much. They're both really smart and have been interested in these fields since they were kids, so it's no surprise."

Impressive, I think. UCLA and Yale? That's super cool. Both of them are colleges that have great English programs, which is what I would like to do. As part of our private middle school's curriculum, we have one guest parent speaker in a particular field come in every month and talk about their chosen career path, and writing-related majors and jobs have always been the most appealing to me. And obviously, Cruise's entire family thinks along the same lines. Not expected, but a happy realization.

"What about you?" I ask. "Which parent are you following? I guess it must be some kind of a competition between them, seeing which one can persuade the last kid to come over to their side."

He laughs. "You definitely aren't wrong. Since we enter high school in a few months, my parents have slowly but surely been intent on introducing me to their fields. You wouldn't believe the number of office visits I've taken or colleagues I've met in the last six months."

I laugh softly at that, imagining Cruise in his big hoodies and sweats at a law firm.

"However, I am definitely thinking about law, criminal law, to be specific. I know it's hard, but I've been pretty into criminal, well, *anything,* ever since I entered middle school. I love doing all those escape rooms and playing those murder mystery games, so I guess that has to count for something. Plus, those crime podcasts are some of my favorite things ever. Sorry, Dad."

I laugh loudly at that. It's a pleasant change to be talking about something academic. Most of my friends tend to stray away from anything related to school when we talk.

"What about you? What are you thinking, if you know at all?" he asks, staring at me intently, like he really wants to know and isn't just asking out of courtesy.

"Ideally, I'd love to work as a technical writer. I enjoy computer science, and I *love* writing, so it would be a great mix between the two. My dad works as a software engineer, and my mom is the editor-in-chief for the local newspaper, so I think it would be a nice mix."

Cruise nods at the end of my little speech. "That's pretty cool. I haven't heard of that career path before, but I'm guessing it has something to do with code and writing?"

I nod at him.

"Super cool. Coders have my respect. That's not easy at all."

A small burst of happiness starts to bloom in my stomach. His words sit well with me. They shouldn't, but they do. I smile at Cruise, and he cracks a grin too.

"Shall we crash my dad's interview setup?" he says, making a grand gesture with his hands.

"Let's do it," I respond. "I'm actually kind of excited. I've been looking forward to this since you told me about it."

"Me too. I just hope he doesn't get annoyed by the two incredibly intelligent middle schoolers who keep bombarding him with questions," Cruise says, cracking a smile.

We end up laughing at that as we make our way to a large room with four large computer monitors and a few microphones. We settle down on the large, cushiony, white couch, setting up the video call to capture both of us in the frame. When the professor joins the waiting room, both Cruise and I jump and look at each other, anticipation glimmering in our eyes.

"You ready?" Cruise asks, a wide smile on his face.

"As ready as I could be," I respond, grinning.

We let the professor into the meeting and for the next hour and a half, chat with him about the mercantilist policies of Britain during the American Revolution. Throughout the interview, I feel my heart beating rapidly as it processes my constant thought: *I'm talking to a professor from Stanford.*

After we finish up our call and wave goodbye to the professor, I fall back on the couch, breathing out shakily.

"That. was. surreal," I say, looking at Cruise.

He looks back at me, his face bright and satisfied. "Agreed. I can't believe that just happened," he says, shaking his head and flopping down next to me. "That was such a great interview, though. I think that we got every piece of information we needed. I haven't learned from an experience more in my whole life. I absolutely *loved* that."

"Dude, *yeah*," I say, smiling again. "Thank you, though. This would not have been possible without you being brave enough to contact him."

"Anytime," he says, nodding. "The professor definitely knew what he was talking about, and I think Mr. Harfateh is really going to appreciate our extra effort."

I nod and grin and then begin to gather my stuff. "Anyways, I want to get a run in before the end of the day today, so I'm going to head out."

Cruise nods at me. "Sounds good. Let me walk you to the door," he says, gesturing toward the direction of the door.

"Thanks," I say.

We fall into a comfortable silence as we walk, the sound of our padding feet muffled by the thick white carpet. I feel nowhere near as uncomfortable and nervous as I did when I first entered his house; his presence is comforting. When we reach the door, I fumble with the locks for a bit before he laughs and gently pushes me to the side to smoothly unlock the door.

"Ah. Yes, perhaps the person living in the house knows how to do that best." I say, slightly embarrassed.

He chuckles and says, "Well, learning experience for you. Hopefully, you watched closely because next time, you're on your own. No help from me. Nope." He raises his hands and pretends to run away.

I laugh, but something he says sticks with me.

"Next time?"

"Yeah, I mean, I thought, well, you're going to come over again to work on the project with me. If you want, of course. I don't, um, mean to push anything on you," he says, his face turning a bit red.

And to my surprise, I find myself saying, "Yeah. I'd love to come over again."

Cruise takes a breath to calm himself down and then responds, "Cool. I'd be happy to have you." He cracks a small grin, and I feel that familiar bloom of happiness in my stomach again.

I smile at him as well, and we stand there for a few seconds before I realize that I should leave before it gets too awkward.

"Well, I should get going. See you soon," I say.

He nods and waves goodbye. I hear the click of the door shutting once I leave his driveway, and I increase my pace. The sun is partially hidden behind a few clouds, but some of its warmth manages to escape through cracks and hit my skin. The sky is incredibly blue where there aren't any clouds, and I watch a pack of migrating geese slowly make their way across the vast, blue expanse. I slow my pace to take in the surroundings, enjoying every second of it. I reach into the back pocket of my jeans, pull out my AirPods, and plug them in, thinking about the past few hours.

It all boils down to one main conclusion: Cruise does not match my friends' descriptions at all.

My friends said that he was rude and condescending. But today, he was genuine and incredibly kind.

My friends said that he was always on edge and that everything set him off. But I thought he was quite possibly one of the chillest people I've met.

My friends said that he didn't care about academics whatsoever. But he seems incredibly focused and wants a successful future.

In sum, I'm thoroughly confused. Cruise today was basically the opposite of what my friends told me, and I don't know what to think.

What about Silke?

What about her interactions with him?

What about that side of him?

A grim look comes onto my face as I think about what he did. That wasn't alright whatsoever, and I know for a fact that he did all of that. What about that side of him?

But what about the side you just saw?

As I walk towards my mom's car, there is only one question echoing through my mind.

Who is the real Cruise?

The dishes in the kitchen clang together as my mom and I finish loading the dishwasher. From the living room comes the loud whirring sound of the vacuum manned by my father. I rinse each dish in the warm running water, and my mom loads everything into the washer. The vacuum shuts off, and my dad walks into the kitchen, leaning on one of the countertops.

"Done with my part, ladies. You guys hurry up now, don't keep the master of chores waiting," my dad says playfully, making a grand, flourishing show with his hands.

My mom and I both laugh.

"Alright, alright, show off," my mom says, shaking her head. "We're about done, so go get your jacket so we can go. Do you know where it is?"

My dad stands there for a few seconds, a thoughtful look coming over his face, one that soon gets replaced by slight embarrassment. It's a running joke in our family that while my dad can code websites and apps within hours, he can never remember where the most basic items are. My mom laughs when she sees his face and shakes her hand in his direction, splashing him with water. My dad yelps when the droplets hit him.

"Oh, silly. In the closet, next to your green *kurta*. Where it has been for the past three years, ever since we moved into this house," my mom explains, shaking her head once more but with a smile on her face.

"Oh, yeah, got it. I knew that. I was just making sure that you did," my dad says nonchalantly, playing his forgetfulness off.

"Oh, of course. Now go get it before you forget where it is again." My mom shoos him away, threatening him with the water on her hands, and my dad walks away laughing.

I look between the two of them, smiling. My parents are best friends and have been ever since they met at UC Berkeley, where both of them went for their undergraduate degrees. They were friends for almost seven years before they started dating, and within a few years, they were married. I've always been an only child, but the dynamic of our family works. My *chacha* and *masi*, who are my parents' siblings, live about twenty minutes away from us, and we visit them and their kids all the time. My family has always made sure that I never feel alone, and I love them for that.

The number of dishes in the sink soon dwindles, and we eventually finish. We dry our hands on one of the orange and white tea towels my mom hangs on our oven handle and gear up for our walk. My dad meets us at the door, and we set off. The weather is slightly chilly today, the wind crisp and cold. Winter is soon approaching, and the greenery around us reflects that— the trees are turning red, orange, and yellow. The leaves on the road make a crunching sound when I jump on them, and my mom soon joins me. We squeal and run in front of my dad as we step on every leaf that comes into sight. Once we tire ourselves out, we fall back and walk with my dad, lapsing into a comfortable silence. Our footsteps are soft on the road, and the wind makes the leaves whip up around us.

"So, Sanah," my mom says, turning to look at me. "How was Cruise's?"

I completely forgot to tell them about what happened at his house.

"Oh, yeah, sorry, I totally forgot about that. It was really fun. The interview was *so* enlightening: I don't think I've ever learned that much from a conversation before. We were able to completely finish transcribing the interview and picking out the relevant quotes. I think that we should have a really solid foundation for our slides by the end of the week."

"That's good to hear! I was putting your laundry in your room earlier and noticed some of the design ideas on your desk. They look great," my dad says, nodding at me. "Although, I did want to ask—what was *he* like? Your mom filled me in about the general hostility your group has towards him and how Cruise hasn't acted in the way your friends painted him."

I look out at the path in front of us, thinking about my answer for a few moments.

"Quite honestly, he was pretty cool. I actually had a pretty good time talking to him. Usually, with my friends, even though they're really nice about keeping me in the loop, I always feel out of place because I never really know what they're talking about. But with Cruise, chatting was natural. I left his house feeling great. We have the same interests, the same work ethic, the same goals—we're a lot more similar than I expected."

Both my parents smile softly, and they beckon for me to continue.

I proceed to tell them about every detail of my time at Cruise's house. As I narrate, the smiles on their faces only get wider, and when I finish, both of them are nodding.

"Wow," my mom murmurs. "His personality is completely different from the tales you've been told by your friends."

"Yeah," I agree, nodding vigorously. "Quite frankly, I had a good time."

"I'm so glad, *beta*," my mom says.

I nod, but my mood dims a bit as I feel a new concern move to the forefront of my mind, one that had started growing ever since I came home from Cruise's house. It's a worrying one, but it simply isn't going away regardless of how much I try to get rid of it.

"Something on your mind, *beta?*" my mom asks, her brows furrowing a little in concern.

Trust my mom to notice that something was wrong. I take a deep breath in, remind myself that running away from problems is never the way to go, and start explaining my dilemma to my parents.

"It's hard for me to admit this, but I felt a lot more akin to Cruise in one afternoon than I have to my friends since we've started hanging out. Prior to today, I'd basically accepted that not being able to contribute to every conversation and feeling a little aloof was something that everyone went through in friendships. But today, after interacting with Cruise for the first time in what seems like *forever*, I felt involved *and* interested in the conversation. I had the same type of conversation with him as I do with you, which was something I had never even expected out of a friend. I'm so used to being on the outskirts with everyone other than Fay and Klyah, with whom I still do feel a tad bit left out, that I had normalized it in my mind."

I let out a shuddering breath, the relief of letting out every anxiety-inducing thought washing over me. My parents slow their pace, glancing at each other and thinking about how to respond. There's complete silence for a few moments, nothing but the occasional cricket chirp and the faint sound of the highway surrounding us. Then, my mom breaks the silence.

"Firstly, thank you for admitting this to us. It isn't easy to be so vulnerable, especially after what you felt before you joined this group of friends."

A feeling of dread fills my stomach. Thinking about the overarching reason for joining my friend group is agonizing, and I try to avoid it as much as I can. However, hearing my mom's words makes me think back to the era before I joined this friend group, the time period that made me realize that I must stay with my friends *no matter what.*

"However, I talked to Silke's mom earlier today and briefly brought Cruise up. Don't worry," my mom quickly clarifies upon seeing my face take on a nervous look. "I was slick with it. But upon hearing about his actions towards Silke, I sort of retract my earlier advice. I do think you should exercise some caution. These friends are important to you, and I think you need more 'evidence' before you decide that Cruise is someone you absolutely prefer to spend time with despite their wishes."

"Agreed," my dad says, nodding. "We all know what it took for you to find your current group friends, and considering their opinion about Cruise, I wouldn't immediately run to build your friendship with him."

As long as you are happy with them. The phrase echoes in my mind.

"True," I say, nodding and looking up at the black sea filled with tiny, white oysters above me. "I'll be careful about how I go about interacting with Cruise."

"Glad to hear it, *beta*," my mom says.

We fall into a comfortable silence after that, feeling the crisp, icy breeze of the Bay Area's October night on our skin. The only sound around is the crunch of the loose tarmac under our sports shoes. The same thought keeps echoing through my mind, the phrase that my mom mentioned: *As long as you're happy with them.*

I am. And I won't do anything to jeopardize that.

Later that night, I've comfortably tucked myself into bed and am just starting to shut off my lights to go to bed when I hear my phone vibrate. I reach over and pick it up, a little surprised when I see a text from Cruise.

> today was fun. glad we were able to get that interview done.

> definitely. tell your dad that his setup is really impressive

> will do. going back to the topic of working together again, i was wondering if you wanted to anytime soon?

I hesitate for a second. I'm not sure if I want to willingly interact with him, especially after the conversation I had with my parents earlier this evening. However, we do need to get a ton of work done. It actually might be a good idea to invite him over because that way, we aren't in any danger of people seeing us outside together.

> definitely. wanna come to my house next sat?

Having him over at my house would give my inquisitive mom the chance to meet him as well, and her advice would be a lot more targeted. Once again, I'm a bit worried about how friendly this action seems, but it's really the best option I have right now.

My phone vibrates, and the lock screen lights up, notifying me that Cruise has responded. Heart pounding a little, I unlock my phone and check his response.

id love to. send me ur addy

I sigh. *Here we go.*

CHAPTER SEVEN

★　★　★

The house is full of hustle and bustle on Saturday. My dad and I collectively clean up the house to get it ready for Cruise's arrival later today, and my mom prepares lunch for the two of us in the kitchen. I take the vacuum upstairs so I can clean my carpets, and after many rounds around the room, I shut it off and collapse onto my bed, tired. I didn't get much sleep last night because I stayed up late doing some homework, and as I sink into the soft covers of my bed, I find my eyes shutting.

A quick power nap, I think, allowing myself to drift off into my dreams.

Ding dong!

The doorbell rings, and my eyes shoot open. I quickly sit up in bed, trying to get my bearings and remember what's going on.

Shoot. Cruise.

I scramble out of bed and frantically smooth the covers to make it seem neat. I rush over to my mirror and groan when I see my tousled hair. I grab a comb and run it through my hair a few times to try to make it look a little better. From downstairs, I can hear my mom's footsteps going toward the door, and I wish I could yell at her to slow down. I turn around in a circle a few times, trying to see what needs to be fixed in my room next.

"Ah, hello, Cruise!" I hear my mom say from downstairs.

His deep voice responds in what seems like a polite way, and I stop for a few seconds to try to hear the conversation.

"Hi, Mrs. Patel. It's wonderful to meet you. Here, I brought something for the family."

Cruise seems to hand something over to my mom, which my mom is ecstatic about, from the exclamations of joy coming from her.

Huh, I think. *A gift? Never seen that from anyone here before.*

I desperately look down at my clothes and then at the door. I don't have time to change, so I go to my mirror and attempt to smooth down the wrinkles. I'm wearing an old, oversized shirt from a camp I attended at Stanford University last summer, along with oversized black sweatpants.

Definitely not my usual look, but I can't really do anything about it now.

I shoot one last panicked look at my appearance and my room before pulling open my door and heading downstairs. With every step I take, my nerves get worse. However, upon seeing the big smile on my mom's face as she speaks to him, I'm slightly relieved, her happy demeanor putting me at ease.

When I walk in, Cruise turns to look my way, and his eyes stop on my face. His eyes trail down and up as he takes me in, and he raises his eyebrows with a smile on his face. I feel my face getting red.

"Oh, hey, Sunny!" my mom says, the use of my childhood nickname distracting me for a second.

"*Mom*, no, stop," I groan, knitting my eyebrows together.

"Sunny, that's a cool name. Like your presence!" Cruise says, laughing.

My mom joins him, and I'm slightly taken aback by his nice comment.

"Thanks, Cruise," I say, a bit surprised.

"What can I say? It's all true," he says, grinning at me.

I somehow find myself smiling back.

"Alrighty, I'll let you two kids get back to work. Sunny's dad and I have to head out to a furniture shop. Will you two be alright alone?" my mom asks, looking between the two of us.

"Yes, Ma, we'll be fine. Go have fun, and don't spend too much money on furniture. I know you," I say, playfully wiggling a finger at her, and she laughs.

"Perfect. I'll finish up the lunch I'm making for the two of you soon, and then you guys can get to work!"

"Oh, Mrs. Patel, there's no need to prepare anything, I don't mean to give you more trouble," Cruise protests, but my mom firmly shakes her head.

"No, it's no trouble at all. What kind of a host would I be if I let my guest leave without eating? Besides, you obviously haven't tasted my *bhindi*. If you did, then you would most definitely not be saying this."

Dread starts to pool in my stomach as my mom talks, and I think back to the way Silke voiced her implicit disgust for my food the one time we did make homemade dishes for my group. I don't want that to happen again. That was humiliating enough, and I feel a chill come over me as I think about it. I have no idea what Cruise thinks about Indian food, but if it's anything along the lines of what Silke thinks, then my mom needs to stop talking right now.

"Sanah, here, take this plate and serve him a sample to give him something to look forward to."

I freeze up a little at my mom's insistence and look between her excited expression and Cruise's amused one.

"No, mom, that's alright. I don't want to force anything on him."

"What are you talking about? I'd love to try some. This seems delicious."

Confusion floods my face, and Cruise notices it instantly as he stands up a little straighter and repeats what he said.

"I'd love to try some, Sanah. Go ahead, serve it to me."

Not completely convinced of his sincerity and still a bit scarred from my experience with Silke, I attempt to postpone the taste test to a time when my mom isn't in the house.

"Can we work first? We can eat after we finish if that's alright?"

"Ugh, fine," my mom says, placing the plate down. She points a finger at me. "He does not leave without eating." My mom then points her finger at Cruise. "You do not leave without eating. Understood? Alright, kids. Have fun!"

My mom quickly saunters out of the room, turning around once to wave goodbye to us. I look over at Cruise and burst out laughing when I see the slightly startled and amused look on his face. He's looking straight at where my mom left, and slowly, he starts to smile before he chuckles and looks at me.

"Your mom rocks," is all he says before he turns around and walks toward his backpack.

At his words, my heart fills with warmth. Anyone who compliments my parents automatically has my approval. None of my friends have ever really shown interest in speaking to or getting to know my parents, so as I walk over to Cruise, I feel great that he seems to care.

"Alrighty, so I've got most of the materials for the poster we need to make. I didn't bring the little things like tape or black pens because I hoped you'd have them," he says, picking his backpack off the floor.

He looks over at me with a questioning glance just to confirm that I do, and I nod at him.

"Perfect. Were you able to start on the slideshow?"

"Not really, I was trying to get some studying in for the chemistry test we have on Monday, but I did create a title slide. Which, I mean, if you ask me, is a lot of work," I say, folding my arms and nodding exaggeratedly.

"Dang. A whole title slide? That's impressive. You know what, I'm gonna quit while I'm ahead and just give you all the credit," Cruise says, backing away with his hands in the air.

I let out a laugh and shake my head. "Alright, yeah, I know. Not much, but I'll work on it more, I promise."

"No worries. Let's get a lot done today. To your room!" Cruise says and starts carrying his backpack out of the living room, acting as though he knows where he's going.

I'm tempted to tell him that he's heading the wrong way, but I purse my lips with a smile. A few moments later, he walks back into the living room, looking at me with an embarrassed look on his face.

"Uh, if you wouldn't mind leading the way please."

★ ★ ★

I lead Cruise up the carpeted stairs, making terribly awkward polite conversation with him as we walk.

"How's your day been?"

"Pretty good. How about yours?"

"Good, just tired."

"Ah, same."

As we enter my room, he says, "Okay, that was horrendous. Never again."

"Okay, yeah," I agree, laughing.

He cracks a grin at me and gestures toward the door.

"After you, Madam," he says in a terrible French accent.

"Ooh, no, bad try," I say, groaning as I walk through the door.

Cruise snickers behind me but goes silent after a moment. I turn around, confused as to why he isn't saying anything, but I realize the reason when I see his face. His eyes are wide, and his mouth hangs open as he takes in my room. He lets out a low whistle as he turns in a full circle.

"Dang, Sunny," he says, meeting my eyes. "You've done well with this."

"Thanks," I say, smiling at him. "This took about six months to complete, but it was well worth it."

I turn to face the room and take it in with him.

The right side of my room has my twin-sized bed with its light blue comforter and a massive mound of pillows, with either blue or white pillow covers. The faded blue stuffed monkey I got when I was two years old lies in the middle of the pillow mound, and it clutches the remote to the golden fairy lights on my wall. Behind my fairy lights is a multi-colored blue mandala tapestry that I made a few years ago at a school event. In the middle of my room, straight ahead, is a large window, under which there is a small ledge on which I spend my free hours reading. A bookshelf is built into the ledge, and it's decorated with all of my favorite books.

In the left corner of my room are my desk and all my study materials. My computer lies half-open, and a few notebooks are scattered around it from doing my math homework, but it's relatively clean other than that. A large bulletin board is pinned onto the wall in front of my desk, and it contains dozens of pages with my notes. The corners are decorated with pictures of my family and vacations that I've taken. On the left side of my desk is a large bookshelf that contains all my textbooks, awards from writing competitions, and my other books that I couldn't fit into my ledge bookshelf. All around my room, I've plugged in various lamps and spread fairy lights just to bring on a more cozy feel. I look over at Cruise once more. He's nodding with a smile on his face, and when he looks at me, I can't help but smile back.

"This is really impressive. I love this."

"Thanks, Cruise," I say, grinning.

"Alrighty, shall we get started?" he says.

"Let's do it," I say, nodding.

Cruise plops down onto the ground and begins to pull out the materials he's brought over while I go to my desk to pull out some tape and black pens. The large board on which we've begun our poster lies in the middle of my faded blue carpet, and I scatter the black pens over it. Cruise sets up his laptop to the side so that we can both see the rough outline for the poster on the screen, and I take a quick picture of it so that I can reference it on my phone. Cruise asks if he can play some music, and I nod, so he puts on a soft pop playlist that fills the room with a coffee-shop-like vibe. We fall into a rhythm, letting the music guide us through the work. The pen softly scratches on the thick paper as we sketch the outlines of the drawings we need for our poster, coupled with the clicking of the keys as we research information for the content of our poster. We make easy conversation, far smoother than before, and laugh and chat as we work. After an hour, I bring out a couple of snacks for us as fuel as we work, and we keep grinding through our work.

"Oh, woah, it's been three hours," I say when I glance up at the clock. I look back at our poster, and the colorful board looks back at me. It's covered with snippets of information, large drawings, and cut-outs of pop-up drawings we created, and I nod, satisfied.

"Wanna take a break?" Cruise suggests.

I smile. "You read my mind."

We get up off the floor and stretch, tight from having sat down for three hours of not moving.

"I'm curious to try the dish that your mom mentioned earlier. Something with a B?" Cruise says, looking at me.

Instantly, I feel my heart start to beat a bit faster. I'm nervous about him trying it: what if he reacts like Silke? My mom isn't here this time, but I still would hate for anyone to say anything bad about it.

"Yeah, *bhindi*," I murmur, looking away in an attempt to dissuade him from pursuing the topic, but he keeps pushing.

"Can we eat some? I'm starving, and it looked delicious."

"Oh. Sure, let's go downstairs," I say, a bit taken aback at his eagerness.

His enthusiasm is a bit reassuring, but I'm still a bit nervous about him trying it. I quickly lead the way out of my room, Cruise following close behind me. *Bhindi* is one of the staple dishes of Indian culture, but there's just something about the way that my mom makes it that elevates it to the level of a fancy, restaurant-like dish. I crave it frequently, and my mom is more than happy to make it because it's healthy.

"What exactly is this dish?" Cruise asks as we walk to the kitchen.

"It's the vegetable Okra stirred in a mix of onions, spices, and various other herbs. Sometimes, my mom adds in tomatoes if we have them too. It's super delicious, but it can get pretty spicy." I look at him with raised eyebrows. "How's your spice tolerance?"

"Uh, low," he says, laughing nervously. "Although I can eat a whole pack of flaming hot Cheetos without my head exploding. Does that help me?"

I laugh, shaking my head. "Nice, but I think you're gonna find that this may take a little more tolerance than that. To preface this, I don't find flaming hot Cheetos spicy."

"Say what?" Cruise stops, and I turn to see him giving me an incredulous look. "You're telling me no watery eyes, no sucking in air, no glasses of water after?"

"Yes," I say, chuckling. "So, basically, good luck."

Cruise shakes his head. "Oh, I'm totally looking forward to this."

We enter the kitchen, and I see the dishes decorated on the long marble island in the middle. The bowl with *bhindi* sits in the middle, sparkling in all its glory. I grab a serving spoon from the large cutlery holder on the side and scoop a spoonful of the dish onto two plates. I open the small box next to the large bowl and take out two *rotis*, or Indian flatbread. I scoop some of the other curries onto the plates as well, and once I finish dishing up the food, I hand one of the plates to Cruise.

"Here," I say as he takes the plate from me. "Pull up a chair to sit. I'll move some stuff around, so we have space to put our plates."

Soon enough, we're seated at the table, ready to dig in. I watch as Cruise stares confusedly at his food for a bit, silently debating how to first go at it.

I laugh and ask, "Can't decide what to eat first?"

"Oh, yeah," he says, looking at me. "It all looks really good. I'm also a little terrified at the whole spice level thing, so I'm debating how soon I should start setting my mouth on fire."

"Oh, please. It's not that bad. I'm overexaggerating. Try it, come on." I rip off a piece of the flatbread, scoop up some of the *bhindi*, and eat it to encourage him to do so himself. The spices of the vegetables hit my tongue, and I immediately go back for seconds.

"Okay. I'm gonna do it."

"Okay, I'm watching. Preferably, I'd be videotaping as well, but my phone's in the other room, and I'm lazy, so you're spared that humiliation."

"Uh, no, my fear is prominent enough. The fact that you feel the need to videotape is worrying. I'm predicting that I will be in a lot of pain."

"Yes, and to speed up that process, *try it.*"

Cruise looks down at the food, takes a deep breath, and begins ripping off a piece of the flatbread. He folds it into a scoop-like shape and uses his spoon to place some of the vegetables inside. He then looks at me, takes a deep breath, and nods, silently saying, *It was nice knowing you, soldier.*

I suppress a smile and solemnly nod back. He then quickly scoops the bite into his mouth and begins to chew. I watch his face as the flavors begin to circulate, my heart beating faster by the second as I wait for his reaction, praying that it will be good.

His eyes widen as he begins to chew more quickly, and when he looks at me, only one word comes out of his mouth: "Woah."

"You like it?" I ask, folding my arms and looking back at him, surprised. He breaks into a smile and nods vigorously.

"That's actually, like, seriously good. It's definitely spicy, but *wow.* So flavorsome."

He rips off another piece of the bread and scoops up more of the vegetable, placing it into his mouth hurriedly. I smile as I see his excitement, my own happiness rising. My friends don't usually come home, and when they do, we usually order out because none of them particularly enjoy Indian food. We learned that the first time, when Silke said my mom's curry was too much for her palette, and most of the others agreed. We never made Indian food for them again. However, Cruise appreciates the food in a way no one else has so far. I stare at him for a few seconds, digesting this, taking in his curly brown hair, his long eyelashes, his bright but watery eyes. *He really is different,* I think. *He's nothing like the person Silke described him to be.*

Cruise looks back towards me and notices me staring. He snaps his fingers in front of my face, and I startle out of my thoughts.

"Earth to Sanah? What's on your mind?"

"Oh, sorry, uh, got stuck on some ideas for the project," I say quickly.

"Forget about the project for a bit. Enjoy this delicious spread. Although, you need to warn your mom that if this is the kind of food that you get to eat, I'm going to be moving in very soon."

"You're welcome anytime. We love feeding people."

He smiles at me and goes back to eating, but a few seconds later, he looks back up.

"Also, could I get a glass of water? You weren't kidding when you said this was spicy. My mouth is about to explode, but I can't stop; it's too good. I'm taking the pain."

I burst out laughing at that and shake my head amusedly as I grab him a glass of rescue.

Half an hour later, we've migrated to the living room, tired out from all the eating. Cruise and I are leaning on a different couch on either end of the set, talking. Willingly.

Never expected to be doing this, I think, as Cruise and I talk about everything from books to writing, from TV shows to hobbies, from future plans to personal stories that have us rolling on the floor with laughter. The sunlight streaming through the window slowly dims, and soon enough, the window is lit up with pink and orange splashes of color.

"Oh, jeez, it's already evening," Cruise says, getting up and slowly walking towards the door to the balcony. "The sky is really pretty today, though."

I slowly break into a grin. "You wanna see a better view?"

He turns back, raising his eyebrows. "There's a better view than this? Lead the way."

We scurry back up to my room, and the second we enter, Cruise gasps, slowly walking towards my window.

He takes a seat on my window ledge and stares out, looking at the painting in the sky. "This is *gorgeous,*" he says, looking back at me and pointing to the view. "You have the best view of the sunset possible. You're higher than all the houses. I can't imagine being able to see this every day."

I walk over to the window ledge and sit on the other side. "Yeah, it's pretty gorgeous, actually. I usually take a break from my work to watch it."

"You're super lucky. We didn't get to see my room, but it's positioned on the worst possible side of the house. My only view is into our backyard, which either has no one in it or my mom mowing the lawn. Not very exciting."

I giggle. "Well, you're free to stare at the sunset anytime you get bored of your own view. Although, I mean, that empty backyard is definitely something I'd pay to see. Sounds *exhilarating.*"

"Shut up."

I crack up, and he joins in, our laughs filling the room with a cozy feeling. The evening has definitely changed my opinion of him. Never, not even in my wildest dreams, did I imagine sitting and talking to him, nor did I imagine that I would actually like it. We have the same hobbies and like the same things. We're more similar than I ever imagined. I haven't had a conversation in which I've been invested since I can remember. While my parents and I talk a lot, there's a difference between talking to your parents and a friend.

Friend, I think. I look at him laughing and smile a little broader. *Yeah, he's my friend now.*

Cruise notices me staring and wiggles his eyebrows. "Like what you see?" he says slyly, making a grand show with his hands and face.

"Gross, shut up. I've only just started to find you tolerable. Don't make me regret my decision."

He laughs and stands up to look around my room, observing all my belongings. I look out of the window again, staring down at the few cars going in and out of the road leading into our street. I scan the road for my parent's car, and when I don't see it, I check my phone to see if I've gotten a message from them.

Grabbing dinner. Let us know if Cruise wants to eat with us; he's free to stay.

"You wanna stay for dinner?" I ask him, still looking at my phone as I type my response to their first message. He doesn't respond immediately, and when I look up to see why, my breath hitches. He has a picture of me and my friends in his hands, and he's staring at it. I stay quiet, unsure of what to say, and the silence fills the room, becoming suffocating after a while. I know he's aware of the fact that I'm friends with people he has history with, but neither of us have really brought it up so far, and I'm not sure how he's going to respond to that. The room is quiet for a few moments before Cruise finally breaks the silence.

"Why are you friends with them?"

Of all things, I wasn't expecting him to ask that, and I don't really know how to respond. I open my mouth and close it, abandoning responses as they fly through my mind.

"I mean, they've been my friends forever. Like, Fay and Klyah have been my friends since basically forever. I have a good time with them, so, I mean, yeeeeaaah."

He still hasn't looked up from the picture, and I sense him turning my words over in his mind, digesting them. My explanation was partly true. I didn't mention the bigger reason, of course. No one knows about that.

Cruise finally looks up from the picture and stares directly into my eyes. His gaze startles me a little, mainly because of how intense it is.

We maintain eye contact for a few seconds, neither of us saying anything, and then he says, "So, not because you really like them or anything."

I do a double-take at his words. "No, I mean, well, yeah, of course, because I like them. I mean, that's a given."

Cruise keeps looking at me, obviously unconvinced. His face is stony and expressionless, but his eyes give everything away. They sharpen ever so slightly, as though instantly wary of me, and surprisingly, I feel my heart sink.

"Okay," he says and places the photograph back on my shelf. He then turns to face me directly, and his whole body posture has changed. He's rigid. "I think I'll go home for dinner. Tell your parents that it was a pleasure meeting them and that I thank them for the food."

He then turns around, picks up his backpack, and walks straight out of the room.

"Wait, Cruise, hold on," I say, getting up quickly and following him.

He's far ahead of me, and I'm confused. What happened? What just changed?

He turns back to look at me as he gets off the stairs. "That's alright,

I'll see myself out. Thanks for having me over," he mumbles as he turns back around.

"Cruise, *wait*," I say more forcefully from the top of the stairs, and he stops.

He looks at me. I look back.

For a few seconds, it's just us standing on opposite ends of the stairs, the few steps between feeling like a thousand miles. The gap between us widens as the seconds tick by.

Too big to close. Too wide to cross.

Yet again.

Finally, he sighs and looks down at his feet. "Look, thank you for having me over. I really enjoyed talking to you, and it was nice to get to know you better."

He looks back up at me as he says this, and our eyes meet. This time, they're less cloudy, but they still seem to be a protective cage surrounding him.

"I would love to get to know you more. I think you're a really cool person, and I really enjoy spending time with you. But, as you probably know, your friends and I don't have the best history, so you'd understand why I feel a little closed off."

I know that I have to clarify this. I don't think either of us is comfortable with going any more in-depth about the situation with my friends quite yet, so

I just leave it at that.

"Look, I understand. I completely do. Sure, I've definitely heard stuff about you and Silke, but that doesn't mean I automatically hate you." I take a deep breath and continue on, my voice shaking ever so slightly. "I think you're a really cool person too, and I would love to hang out with you more too. I do like my friends, but my interactions with you are what really determine whether I continue my friendship with you, not what they say. And I hope that you can do the same by basing your opinions on me by looking at who I am rather than who I hang out with."

Cruise stares at me for a few seconds, his face completely neutral. Heart in my throat and praying that the advice my mom gave me works, I wait.

"Alright, point taken. Let's give this friendship a shot."

It takes a few seconds for me to digest what he says.

"Wait. Really?" I ask, a little in shock.

"Yeah," he says, smiling a little. "I think you're really cool, and I'd like to be friends with you. I'm taking your advice and not judging you based on your friends. And I hope that you mean what you say when you say that you aren't basing your opinions on me off of your friends' experiences."

"I'm not," I say, shaking my head. "But, okay. Cool. Yeah, let's do this."

"Cool. Sounds good. Alright, well, I should head out," Cruise says, smiling.

We walk towards the door in silence, and I wave goodbye to him, shutting the door quietly after he leaves. Happiness blooms in my stomach as I walk toward my room. I'll do anything to stay with my friends because I *need* a group. I know what happens when I don't have one. But despite that, despite knowing this may all blow up in my face, Cruise gives me a shot at pure friendship, one that isn't based on necessity. Even though it's scary to admit that maybe that is what my friendship with my group is based on.

I'll balance both of them together. I'm going to make this work. If it means I need to avoid him when I'm around my friends and say a couple of white lies, then so be it. I'm not losing anyone.

CHAPTER EIGHT

★ ★ ★

"Silke, no way, he didn't actually!"

I hear my friends before I see them, their screams echoing through the hallways. I turn the corner and see them gathered around our main table, clustered around Silke, excited looks on their faces. The tall veranda they're seated under provides shade from the beating sun outside, and there's no one else seated around us. People know to give us our space. Each of them has their phone out and is pointing, tapping, scrolling on them, their fingers moving so fast they're practically blurry. I hesitate behind the corner that I'm watching them from. One side of me really wants to see what's going on, but the other knows that I probably won't understand it anyways.

"Boo," says someone from behind me, and I yelp, turning around with a jump.

Cruise is standing there, leaning on the wall in a big blue hoodie and black sweatpants.

"Bro, you scared the bejeezus out of me," I say, shoving him.

He laughs, stumbling backward. "You're very welcome. Now, care to explain why you're standing behind a corner staring at your friends?"

"Uh." I stare at him, and he raises an eyebrow at me. "Ok, moving on, *so*," I say.

"Ah, changing the topic, I see," Cruise says, smiling and looking down. "No worries, alright. Let's go; I'll walk you to class."

He grabs my backpack and pulls me backward, and I yell at him to stop, stumbling and falling behind him.

"Cruise, yo, wait!"

He laughs and pulls me upright. I grumble at him under my breath but end up with a smile on my face. We walk toward my first-period classroom, chatting casually, avoiding talking about the tension of yesterday.

"So, how was the rest of your weekend?" Cruise asks.

"It was good. I ended up finishing the last of the slideshow at home, so just take a look at it whenever you can. That way, we can cross one task off our list."

"Sounds good. Thanks for finishing that—"

"*Sanah?*"

A chill runs down my spine as I recognize the voice. I hear her footsteps come closer and closer, radiating furiousness. Cruise's face drops like a stone, and he stares right at me, both of us thinking the exact same thing: *Crap.*

"Sanah, what on earth are you doing?" the voice demands, and I turn around to see Silke standing there, arms crossed and a furious look on her face. "You're talking to him? Really?"

"Silke, wait—" Cruise tries to cut in, but Silke shoots him a murderous look, and he falls silent.

"Don't speak to me, you jerk. Don't even look at me," she says, spitting her words at him. She then turns back to me. "Yeah? Explanation, *Sanah?*"

"Sanah, look, we're just talking."

"And *why* are you talking? Do you have no sense of loyalty?" Silke shakes her head, giving me an incredibly dirty look.

I'm left speechless, unable to think of a response to her. The people around us have grown quiet as well, looking between the two of us. Everyone knows to keep quiet when Silke is blowing up. Silke's eyes continue to bore into me, demanding an answer. She raises an eyebrow, and I force myself to speak.

"Silke, he's my partner for my project. I was just talking to him because of that."

"Why? You can work on it without speaking outside of class. Better yet, just let him do everything." Silke pauses to look straight at Cruise, and says in a chilling voice, "He's proven that he can do a lot on his own already."

Cruise visibly shrinks into himself, and I'm in shock. Straight to his face? I do want to stand up for Cruise, but I remember: *Keep it down.* I take a deep breath, swallow hard, and nod. Nod hard.

Out of the corner of my eye, I see Cruise whip his head towards me, astonished at the fact that I've let this slide. But he won't understand. No one will.

"Whatever, Sanah. I'm mad. We'll figure this out later," Silke mutters, turning around and walking away from the two of us.

My heart sinks. I let Silke walk away, not saying anything. It wouldn't do me any good to say anything to her right now anyway. She just wouldn't listen.

"Yikes," he says slowly after a few moments of silence between the two of us.

"Yeah," I say, trying to slow my racing heart.

I look up at Cruise and see a tinge of sorrow in his eyes, and I instantly feel bad for not saying anything.

"Look, I'm sorry for not saying anything, but practically, I need to stay in their good books. They're my friends. Plus, considering everything that has happened between the two of you, I guess you did deserve that," I sigh.

He opens his mouth to say something at that but seems to decide against it and just nods.

"Yeah, I guess. Whatever. I hope stuff is fine between the two of you."

He walks away, his dejected shoulders making it clear that he's bothered by what just happened, and the uneasy feeling in my stomach deepens. Is he just saying it to get over the conversation? Is he actually alright with what happened? Did I just mess it up?

After math, I quickly find Silke to make things right with her. She's surrounded by our friends as usual, but I force her out. She protests, but I give her a hard look, and surprisingly, she falls quiet. I pull her towards an empty part of the locker-plastered hallway, and she crosses her arms.

"Yes?"

"I'm sorry about earlier, Silke. It was never my intention to make you feel as though you were being betrayed. Cruise and I were truly only talking about the project. I'd never do anything to make you feel bad. I'm sorry."

Silke looks at me for a bit and then sighs, cracking a smile that looks more like a grimace. "Of course, no worries. We're good. Just try not to let it happen again. Come on, let's go back."

She doesn't apologize for the scene she made, not that I expect her to.

She's not one to accept her mistakes. As we walk back, I catch Cruise walking across the lawn, and we make eye contact. Breath held, I shoot him a small smile, hoping that he responds well. He looks between me and Silke, and it seems as though he's debating how to respond. My stomach sinks a little. What if the spark of our friendship died?

Then, he smiles back: a small one that disappears almost instantly as he turns away, presumably so that Silke can't see, but it's enough to lift me up. Happiness rolls over me when I realize that I didn't screw it up. He's dealt with Silke in the past, so he knows the stakes, and that's a relief for me.

Maybe this might work after all.

CHAPTER NINE

★　★　★

The gravel crunches under the tires of my mom's car as she pulls up in front of Silke's house. I bounce my leg excitedly, my sleepover bag bouncing up and down with the quick movement of my leg.

"I'll pick you up whenever you call me tomorrow, okay?" says my mom, parking the car and looking over at me.

I nod my head and look over at Silke's house. It gives off a sinister feel, looming over me and casting large shadows over the ground. Silke's house has always looked intimidating; she hates it when we do this, but we always call her house haunted. She doesn't like thinking that any aspect of her life is anything but perfect, which makes sense, but can get a bit overbearing at times.

"Thanks, Mom. I'll see you tomorrow."

I give my mom a quick hug and then open the car door and step out, slinging my sleepover bag over my shoulder. When I slam the car door shut, the noise echoes through the street. As my mom drives away, I practically bounce toward Silke's door. She invited us all over for a sleepover, and I spent the whole week waiting for this moment.

I approach her private estate, instantly recognizing her tall, white, modern house. I step onto the polished, clean steps of Silke's front porch and take a deep breath as I ring the doorbell, the silence from her house becoming slightly suffocating.

Almost instantly, the door flies open, and I'm greeted by the makeup-plastered face of Silke's mom.

"Oh, *hello* darling, do come in," she croons.

The powerful smell of her fruity perfume hits me hard, and my eyes begin to water from the effort it takes to keep my cough in. The living room that she's standing in has tall, *tall* ceilings and two diamond chandeliers. There are flowers everywhere—on the table in the foyer, on the living room table, and near the shoe rack. The furniture is all a bright, blinding white, and I turn away from it, looking back at Silke's mom.

"Hi, Ms. O'Brien," I say, my voice a little raspy.

I unzip my bag and rummage through it for a few moments to pull out the small gift bag that my mom insisted I take. It's a cultural tradition of ours to give each host a gift, and I hand her the small bag, which has a bottle of perfume. *Okay, maybe this wasn't the best gift,* I think to myself, giggling internally.

"Here you go. Thank you for hosting."

She exclaims with delight and quickly pulls out the perfume I've given her. "Thank you, darling. This is wonderful."

She opens the stopper and spritzes herself a few times (well, more than a few times). I take a step back to prevent my airway from being hopelessly overwhelmed with even more chemicals and smile at her.

"This is a lovely smell, dear; I think I have a similar one from Gucci that smells the exact same. It's a wonderful thought, though!"

She smiles at me and places the perfume on a side table from where I'm sure she's never going to pick it up again. I sigh quietly. *Like mother, like daughter.*

"The girls are in Silke's room, darling. Toodle-oo!"

Ms. O'Brien makes a shooing action with her hand and turns away, humming softly to herself. I turn around and begin to navigate my way through Silke's huge house. Silke's sister is an executive at one of the largest tech companies in the Bay Area, and she gives half her income to Silke and her mom. Silke told us that her father left when she was eight years old, but luckily, her sister was just graduating from Dartmouth University when it happened. Elowen took on multiple jobs to put herself through business school and graduated a few years later with the highest honors. She's been living and working in San Francisco ever since, but she still supports the family. I've met her a few times, and I think she's one of the coolest people to exist. Even though she and her family have been through so much, she remains bubbly and cheerful, with a constant positive outlook on life.

Silke and her mom are quite different: they tend to put on a rather overconfident demeanor. However, even though it may get a little annoying at times, it's understandable. For two people who have gone through so much in life, sometimes, that's needed.

I hear the shrieks and laughter from my friends get closer and closer as I walk through the large, high-ceilinged hallways of her house, and I feel my heart speed up a little bit from the anticipation. I pass by empty room after empty room before I finally reach Silke's room, which has its door shut and light and music oozing out of the crack below it. I knock on the door.

"Come in!" I hear Silke's voice say.

I push open the door, taking in her iconic walls. Silke loves polaroids, and she's stuck the hundreds of polaroids she takes in perfectly aligned rows on her walls. Any extras go on the ceiling, which is currently half-full. She has bean bags *everywhere*: she doesn't even have a desk in her room because she works in the study office she has downstairs. Each person in my group has sat down on one. I excitedly greet all of them, laughing loudly as Fay and Klyah jump up from their beanbags and tackle me to the floor with excited looks on their faces.

An hour later, I'm seated next to Fay and Klyah, arms tangled with theirs. Chatter fills the room, along with the smell of pizza. Silke's mom forgot that I don't eat pork and ordered three boxes of pepperoni pizza. I had predicted this, though, so I'd eaten dinner before I got there. The last time I came over, she had ordered steaks for everyone and forgot that I don't eat any because of my religion. I had stayed at the table, stomach grumbling, tapping my foot, and waiting to go back home so I could eat the paneer my mom had promised me as a reward for getting through the night. I quietly chew on the trail mix I had packed as a snack and listen to the rest of the girls talk. I don't really have anything meaningful to add to the conversation topic of "hottest male rapper," but the conversation is entertaining, so I stay engaged and laugh at the funny responses.

When I finish my trail mix, I get up, but Silke yells, "Where are you going? Bored of us?"

"No, just throwing this away," I say, holding up my empty bag.

"Bet she's going to text Cruise," someone calls out, and the rest of the girls laugh.

Silke's face turns sour, and I look behind me to see who said it, a frown on my face. Not funny.

"I hope she isn't. We already know that that would be outright betrayal, don't we?" Silke looks at me pointedly, and I nod.

"Of course. I haven't spoken to him since a few days ago. We only talk about the project," I say, attempting to satiate Silke and trying to get the dread in my stomach to dissipate.

"Good. Now sit back down. We have to decide what we're going to do tomorrow. Gimme, Sanah." she says, snatching the trail mix bag out of my hand.

She deposits it into her trash bin while simultaneously pushing me back to my spot in the circle. I stumble a bit, smiling slightly, and then plop down.

"Alright, suggestions, ladies?"

"Can we go to the record store? Tyler the Creator just released a new album, and I *need* his new vinyl," Addy says from beside me, stretching her hands above her head.

"That's at the mall, though. We won't be able to fit everyone in the car," Fay says, frowning.

"Plus, we went last week after school," Silke says. Then, her eyes widen, and she looks over at me, an apologetic look on her face. "Oh, sorry, Sanah.

I totally forgot you didn't come. I wouldn't have mentioned it otherwise. We weren't sure if you were on a practice run or not."

"No worries," I say, forcing a grin onto my face.

Silke nods and returns to the conversation while I, once again, feel the familiar emotion of being-left-out-of-everything creeps into my chest. I know that I was running, but I would have appreciated at least being asked. Who knows if I would've been able to make time that day?

Is that unreasonable? I wonder. *Maybe it's unreasonable. I'm not sure.*

The girls keep shouting out ideas, but one of my own keeps echoing through my mind. I haven't been to one in a long time, and since the girls are interested in cute picture spots, this might be something that catches their interest too.

"What about we go to a bookstore?" I cut in, and everyone turns to look at me, the noise dying down. I swallow hard and continue on. "We can go to the one nearby and then get lunch after. We can take cute pictures too!"

The girls are silent. Some of them seem open to the suggestion, but most are staring at Silk with neutral expressions. I turn to look at Silke to see what her response is. She has a confused look on her face, as though she can't really believe that I suggested something that seems so … outrageous?

I look back at Fay and Kly, and their faces have turned into mirrors of hers. As I look around the circle, most girls have similar looks of disapproval, even those that initially seemed open to the idea. Surprised, I sit up straight and untangle my arms from Kly and Fay's, especially surprised at their silence, considering how much they like books.

"That's … *one* option," I hear Silke say, and I turn to see her looking at me with a slightly condescending look in her eyes. "But—and I don't mean to be blunt—you're honestly the only one here who likes to read."

Fay and Klyah are silent, and I shoot both of them a quick look of confusion. *Why aren't they saying anything?*

"It's sort of a lame hobby. No offense," Silke says, trying to look apologetic.

I know she doesn't mean it, though. She never means it.

Humiliation and embarrassment turn over in my stomach.

"No, totally understood. We can do something else."

"Yay! Sorry, Sanah, it's nothing against you." she says, "Anyways, where were we?"

As the other girls begin to talk again, I try to stop the tears from filling my eyes. Once again, I've been shot down for trying to put out an idea that I wanted. It's never good enough for them. *I'm* never good enough for them. I look down, fidgeting with my hands, trying to control my slowly increasing breathing. Fay and Klyah aren't looking at me, their hands folded in their lap, and my hurt increases. Silkes's constant, implicit comments always stab deeper and deeper, but it hurts when I know that even the friends I have in this group aren't going to support me. Fay and Klyah just showed that they would always choose Silke, regardless of how hurt I might feel.

Calm, Sanah. You must do this. You must stick with them. This friendship is worth the bad times. Remember what happened to you without them.

I know this. I must.

But it hurts.

And for the first time in a long time, I let myself feel hurt.

★ ★ ★

Later that night, I'm surrounded by the soft breaths of the nine other girls in my group, all fast asleep. I turn over to my side, unable to force myself to shut my eyes. My mind is too active. I reach out, pat the ground a few times to find my phone, find it, and pull it towards me. *1:11 AM,* it reads. I can't remember the last time I stayed up this late. I unlock my phone and begin to scroll through Instagram, liking people's posts and looking through their stories. The conversation with Silke from earlier has remained in my mind, her comments echoing off the walls of my brain.

Problem.

Lame.

Boredom.

I suppose this is what I represent to them.

But I guess I'm alright with being this to them if it means I can avoid the feeling that arises when I'm without them.

The icky feeling in my stomach triples and I open my messages and start writing my mom a quick text.

> Can you pick me up early tomorrow? Not feeling super great

I send her the text and hope that she isn't too worried. She knows what I've been through too, but I don't want to further concern her.

I wait for my mom to respond and start writing her a second message when another text distracts me for a moment. I go back to the list of conversations, and I'm surprised when I see a text from Cruise. He's sent me a picture of something, and when I open it, I can't help but laugh. An image of *bhindi* and *roti* fills up the screen, with a message from Cruise right below.

> Not as good as ur mom's but still delicious

I break into a huge smile. Briefly glancing around to make sure none of the other girls are awake, I text him back.

> omg. cannot believe you ordered some. Where did you even get it from?

He starts typing back immediately after I send the message.

> Scoped out a place. Found some other dishes too. My

mouth is on fire though.

Expected. We need to build up your spice tolerance. Don't
worry, a couple of chillies should do the job.

Ay. That doesn't sound fun. Oh well, if it means I can eat
this food more often, I'm all for it.
What are you up to?

At a sleepover with my friends.

And you're texting me?

Everyone's asleep, haha

You're still awake? Is everything alright?

There it is again. The tinge of joy in my stomach when I realize that
someone actually cares.

Here's the thing: I like my friends. I do. Most of the time, I have a
good time with Fay and Klyah whenever we hang out. I'm always greeted
excitedly by the rest of the girls. Even Silke, whenever she isn't a total jerk,
shows that she cares. But I'm only able to see the good sides of them because I
put on a demeanor that fits with the group. I pretend to be excited about topics
that I don't know anything about. I quiet down when my friends don't think
the things I talk about are interesting enough, so they don't think I'm boring.
I'm not natural in front of them, but I'm so desperate for friends after what
happened after the last time I was alone that I was alright about changing

myself to become someone that they wanted me to be.

But I'm exhausted. I'm exhausted from being something that I'm not. It's not like changing myself does any good: I still feel left out, I still can't contribute, I still can't really be friends with them. A fake demeanor can only facilitate friendships to a certain extent, and I've reached that point.

I may have friends. But maintaining those friends is exhausting. And realistically, I'm not happy with them.

But Cruise makes me happy. In fact, his friendship makes me happier than I've been in all my years of being with my friend group.

So, I text him back.

nope.

Aw. Why? You okay?

not really. they were talking about plans for tomorrow and
i suggested going to a bookstore and they basically said i
was stupid for suggesting it.

No. That's horrible of them
wait. Them or Silke?

I smile, rolling my eyes. Of course he could figure it out.

yeah, silke. but the rest of the girls went along with it, fay
and klyah too.

aw man, i'm sorry sunny.
Don't feel too down though. They don't get you.

124

Bookstores are awesome.

I smile at the screen.

thank you. yeah i was feeling down for a bit, but i feel a bit
better now.
thank you :)

I'm glad.
What are you doing tomorrow?

I smile slightly. Random question, but I'm happy to answer.

nothing. i think i'm gonna go home early because i don't
feel super great after today. i don't really want to hang out
with them tomorrow.

Aw, I'm sorry. Don't feel too down. It isn't worth it.

We text back and forth for a bit, talking about his plans for the next

day, and when the clock strikes 2 AM, I feel a wave of tiredness hit me.

okay, i'm going to bed. i'm exhausted all of a sudden.
i think i texted u a bit too much

ay. mind it
I'm kidding lol. Sleep well!

thank you. goodnight!

CHAPTER TEN

★ ★ ★

Ijolt awake, the headphones I plugged in my ears before falling asleep, blaring a piano tone through my head. I pull them out, breathing hard. Not the best awakening.

I look around me, trying to get a sense of where I am before remembering that I'm stuck in Silke's house. I check my phone to see what time it is. *6:32 AM.* I breathe in deeply, stretching my sore muscles. I make out the faint outlines of the sleeping girls around me and slowly lift myself from the ground, making sure not to accidentally step on anyone. My bag had remained packed for the most part, as I had arrived in my PJs and hadn't really planned to unpack anything else. What would I even take out? My books? *Ha, as if,* I think. *I'd probably get kicked out.*

I tiptoe over the scattered sleeping bags, grabbing my packed backpack. I glance at my phone and see a text from my mom, letting me know that she's on her way to pick me up. I pull on the jacket that I brought and quietly open Silke's door, making sure to avoid the creaky floorboard. My feet pad on the floor as I walk towards the front door. I pass Ms. O'Brien on my way out and see her passed out on the couch, an empty wine glass on the table next to her. My mom would have sent her a text earlier alerting her to my aching stomach, for which reason I had to leave early. The door creaks open as I pull on the handle, and the cold morning air hits me harder than I expect it to. I shiver and pull my jacket tighter around me with the one free hand I have. I see my mom's car pull into the long driveway of the house and speed-walk over to her.

"Hi, *beta*," she says as I enter, wincing and laughing as I bump my head on the car door. "You okay?"

"Yes, for the head bump, not really for the sleepover," I say, rubbing my head with my hand.

"Want to tell me what happened?" my mom says, starting to drive. "We can go get croissants and coffee at that cute little shop you like."

"Thanks, Ma, but I think I want to go home and sleep. I didn't get very much last night," I say, yawning and stretching my hands out over my head.

"You didn't get much sleep? Ms. Sleeps-at-10-everyday?" my mom says, grinning at me.

"Ha ha. Very funny. But I am exhausted."

"Was it the other girls that kept you up?" my mom asks as she fiddles with the radio, turning on the classical music radio station.

I turn a little red. "No, it was Cruise."

We come to a stop at a red light, and my mom turns to give me a surprised look. "Cruise? Why?" she says, a small smile on her face.

I turn redder. "We were texting until pretty late. He texted me a picture of some Indian food he bought yesterday, and we continued to talk after that for a while," I say, looking down at my hands in my lap.

"That's nice, *beta*. I'm glad. However, I do want to ask: why did you want me to pick you up early? Is everything alright?"

My mom says this as we come to a stop at another red light, and she looks at me, concern and worry flooding her face. As I look back at her, I can't bring myself to tell her the truth. I don't think my mom would be open to letting me hang out with my friends as much if I told her the truth about what happened. But even though I don't like these girls, I can't let go of them. And while that decision does come back to stab me in the back at times, it's one I must make.

"Yes, everything's good," I reply, unable to look her in the face. I stare straight ahead of me instead. "They were just going shopping, and I didn't feel like going to the mall today."

I can tell my mom knows that I'm not being honest. She frowns a little and purses her lips.

"Are you sure that's all?" she asks, focusing on the road again as the light turns green.

I look down at my hands in my lap again, breathing deeply.

"Yes, that's all."

As we pull into the driveway of my house and I get out of the car, saying a quick hello to my dad, who is heading out to do the groceries, all I can think about is the fact that I had to lie to my mom about this in order to stay with them. I can't remember the last time I lied to my mom. I dump my sleeping bag in my room and quickly wash my hands before I jump straight into bed, pulling the covers over my head. As sleep washes over me, the last thing I think to myself is, *Is staying with my friends really worth it?*

A shaking sensation forces me awake after what seems like just a few seconds.

"*Beta,* wake up; it's noon already. You've been asleep for four hours."

"Yeah, yeah, I'm up," I sleepily mumble back, turning onto my other side and diving straight back into sleep.

Before I can, my mom pulls the covers off my head, and the bright sunlight streaming in through my window hits my eyelids, eliciting a hiss from me.

"Ugh, fine," I grumble, sitting up in my bed and rubbing my eyes. I squint. "Did you really have to turn on every single light in my room, along with letting the sun blind me?"

My mom laughs. "Yes. You wouldn't get up otherwise. You know that."

"True," I respond, flopping back down in bed, stretching, and yawning loudly.

"Oy, no going back to sleep. Get up and get ready to go out. There's a surprise coming your way in about an hour."

I immediately sit up. "A surprise? What? What is it?"

My mom shakes her head, making a zipped lips motion. I throw her a dirty look, and she laughs. "It wouldn't be a surprise then, would it? Do you have anything planned for this afternoon?"

"No, not anymore. I was going to the mall with the girls, but obviously, that's not happening. I also finished all my homework yesterday so I could go out, so I'm strangely free today."

"Perfect. Go on, get ready. You'll see your surprise soon enough," my mom says, sauntering out of the room with a smile on her face.

I hear her humming as she walks down the stairs, and I'm immediately filled with excitement. My parents give me the best surprises, and I'm pumped. I jump out of bed and go straight to the bathroom to shower and get ready. Half an hour later, I'm seated at my dresser, dressed in a half-sleeved, tight-fitting lavender top and a pair of straight-leg jeans, putting on a pair of white studded earrings and a matching necklace. I spray a lavender-scented perfume on myself, twist my hair up, and hold it in place with a purple hair claw. I quickly check my phone to see what the weather is like and grab a purple embroidered jacket as I head out of my room when I see that it's going to be chilly. I head down the stairs and into the dining room, where my mom and dad are waiting.

"You look super nice!" my mom says as she folds laundry.

My dad nods. "Yes, I remember buying that jacket," he says with a smile. "Do you remember what happened that day?"

"Ah, yes," I say, laughing. "We were at the Gilroy Outlets, and even though it was raining cats and dogs, since we drove three hours, I was determined to get the jacket. I ran through the rain to that vintage store and stood in line for 30 minutes." I shake my head, smiling. "I was stubborn, wasn't I?"

My dad raises his eyebrows at me. "*Was?* Hmm, I'd say you're still pretty stubborn."

"How dare you!" I exclaim, pulling my face into an affronted look and placing a hand on my chest.

My parents laugh, and I drop my act, laughing along with them. The ringing of the doorbell distracts me, and I turn towards the door, trying to look at it.

"Who's at the door?" I ask, confused, looking at them with a questioning look on my face.

My parents simply look at each other, small smiles on their faces, and I'm immediately wary.

"Uh, this is not helping me. In fact, I'm terrified right now. What chaos have you guys been stirring up?"

"Oh, please, you are so overdramatic," my mom says, playfully rolling her eyes at me. She makes a shooing gesture with her hands and says, "Go on, open it!"

I back out of the kitchen, maintaining eye contact with my parents. I turn around once I'm completely out and speed-walk to the door. I quickly pull the door open when I reach it, and my jaw drops when I see who's on the other side.

"*Cruise?*"

He sheepishly waves, shoving both hands into his pocket afterward.

"Hey."

I stand there for a few seconds, my mouth open, hand still on the door.

Cruise shifts uncomfortably and lifts his hand to rub the back of his neck.

"To reassure you, I'm not a stalker, I swear," he says. "I called ahead and asked if I could do this with you."

"Do … what?" I ask hesitantly.

"Take you to a bookstore."

It takes a few seconds for his words to sink into me, and when they do, I have to take a step back. I haven't had a friend do something like this for me in a really long time. Ever, if I think about it.

"I …" I start, unsure of what to say.

His face immediately falls. "Oh, I'm sorry. We don't have to do it if you don't want to. You just seemed really down based on our conversation yesterday, and I thought you would like it if we did this," he says hastily, face turning red.

"No! No, please, stay. I'd love to do this," I say quickly, putting out a hand to stop him from leaving. "I'm just taken aback. In a good way, of course. This is all new for me."

"What is? Bookstores or, uh, me?" he says, confused but with a relieved look coming onto his face.

"Both." I take a deep breath. "I can't remember the last time someone did something I wanted to do."

His face drops into a sad look. "Aw, I'm sorry about that." He takes a step towards me but then thinks better of it and steps back. "Well, that's what I'm here for. We could go over to the downtown area nearby and hang out for a couple of hours."

I smile at him, feeling the first sparks of true happiness that I've felt in a really long time.

"Cruise, thank you so much. This really means so much to me; you have no idea."

He smiles back. "Of course. Anytime."

I hurry back up to my room to gather some money and a small backpack, a huge smile on my face. I'm glad that he sees me in the same way that I see him. And while Silke and the others may not approve of my friendship with him, quite frankly, I don't think I care anymore.

On my way back to the front door, I pass by my parents, still seated around the dining table. I quickly go over to them and give them a hug. "Thank you," I whisper.

They look back at me and smile, nodding. I run back to the front door, where Cruise is waiting and looking at his phone. He puts it away when he notices me coming.

"Ready?" he asks, eyebrows raised and hands in his pockets.

I smile at him and nod. "Ready."

★　★　★

"Have fun, kids!" my mom says, waving at us as she drives away, and we wave back.

"Okay, so I know that there's a Barnes and Noble a little further down. Let's go there?" Cruise asks, looking in that direction.

I furtively smile, shaking my head. "Nah, Barnes and Noble is great, but that's not where we're going to go. Let me show you a real treat."

I start walking, gesturing to him to follow along, and he speed walks to join me.

"Here's hoping you aren't taking me to some random alleyway to murder me. I'm putting all my trust in you right now," he says, playfully punching me in the arm.

"Oh, please," I say, laughing. I smirk at him. "If I was going to murder you, I'd make sure to do it in a much more polished way. Alleyways are too dirty for my liking."

"Oh, please, do enlighten me. Will you be flying me out to your New York suite to carry out the deed? Or is that not fancy enough for you?" Cruise says in a British accent, straightening up and acting royal. I roll my eyes, my smile growing.

"Ah, you seem rather eager to be slaughtered."

"Of course! If it means being witness to your elegant tactics, then yes, please."

I shove him, and he stumbles to the side, laughing. We continue chatting as we walk down the bustling streets. Children shriek as they chase after each other in front of their parents, who lazily call out to them, too relaxed to care. Most of the restaurants are full of customers, and the smell of food drifts out from them, making my stomach grumble. Cruise must hear it because he laughs and points to a restaurant nearby. "Wanna get something to eat?"

"Let's go after," I say. "I really want to show you this bookstore; plus, they have free samples of fudge."

Cruise's eyes widen, and he drops his hand, grabs mine, and pulls me forward, walking much faster than he was before.

"See, it would have helped if you had mentioned this before. Let's go, slowpoke; I want chocolate. I also don't know where we're going, but you can guide me from behind because I wanna *goooo*."

I laugh, falling after him as he continues to pull me. We run together for a few moments before I pull back on his hand, stopping him.

"Hey! Wait, it's right here."

He comes to a stop and raises his eyebrows when he sees the store we've stopped in front of.

"Are you sure this is a bookstore?" he asks, raising his eyebrows.

I see why he's confused. The front window of the store is covered in leaves, vines, and greenery.

"It looks more like a garden store than a bookstore. And I was right. You *are* taking me to some obscure location to murder me. Nobody will be able to see anything past these leaves."

I laugh loudly. "Oh my gosh, abandon the thought that I am a murderer. Just come. You'll see soon enough."

I start walking towards the entrance of the store, and he follows close behind, looking slightly wary. But once I push the front door open, he gasps.

"No way. This is sick."

I smile, taking in what he sees. Rows of bookshelves line a beautiful and precisely created garden. Tiles line the ground in front of the shelves, and plants of all kinds fill in the gaps between. The ceiling is a painting of moss, and photo spots with carefully constructed plant backgrounds line the walls.

"Woah," I hear Cruise say.

I turn to look at him. His mouth is wide open, as are his eyes, and he's looking all around him, taking in the green ocean we're in.

"Dude. This is awesome." He looks back at me. "How on earth was this made?"

"A *lot* of hard work," comes a voice from behind me, and I turn to smile at the middle-aged man with kind green eyes and blond hair walking over to us.

He's dressed in an apron that says, *Nature and books belong to the eyes that see them* on it and is wearing brown garden boots.

"Hi, Ed," I say, waving at him.

"Hello, Sanah. Glad you're back and with a friend this time!" Ed says cheerfully, shaking my hand.

"Yeah, it definitely has been a while. School took a toll on the visits," I say, knowing that I'm lying.

Cruise must pick up on it, too, because he gives me a look that I pretend not to notice. We both know that Silke is the reason I never get to come. I'm too busy going shopping with them to have any time left to visit stores.

"Well, no worries, you're here now. Feel free to show your friend around the store," Ed says, smiling at Cruise. "Oh, and of course, there's fudge in the back." Cruise perks up at this, and Ed laughs. "Ah, yes, the traditional fudge-lover. Buy some books too! Reading and chocolate always go well together."

"Yes, sir," Cruise says, smiling. "I'd love any recommendations."

"Ay," I say, shooting him a look. "I will guide you. Ed will steal you away as he talks about his love for books."

Ed laughs at that. "She's right. You do have your personal book guide standing right next to you."

"Oh, you flatter me," I say, laughing. I look over to Cruise. "Shall we browse?"

He nods vigorously. "Let's browse."

"Be careful not to step on the plants," I say to him as we walk over to the first row of books.

Cruise is stumbling after me, trying to make his way through the narrow entrances to each row.

"I am too clumsy for this. This is not my forte," Cruise says, yelping as he almost trips over a box of stickers left on the floor.

I giggle, shaking my head as I lead the way. We walk through the non-fiction section, browsing the shelves. Cruise picks out a few biographies and stacks them in his hand, and I'm impressed.

"Dang, you read biographies? That's cool. I never had an interest in them."

He moves a little closer and whispers, "No, I'm just stacking them in my hand so that he doesn't think I'm only here for the fudge."

I chuckle, shaking my head. "Oh, jeez. Don't worry. I'm sure we will find a book that you *actually* want to read."

As we turn the corner, the lined-up plates of fudge come into view, and Cruise immediately grins.

"Hold, please," he says, dumping the stack of books into my arms and rushing to the table.

I start laughing hard when he docs that.

"Okay, have fun. I'm gonna go browse some more."

Cruise waves his hand at me as he remains turned toward the fudge table, and I softly laugh. I walk into the next aisle and sigh as I recognize my favorite row of books: the thriller and mystery section. I stack Cruise's books on one of the discard bins that Ed has set out and walk into paradise. My eyes scan the book titles, looking for the one I had come for, but I continually get distracted by other interesting books that I've been wanting to buy for a while. I pick them out, read their summaries, place them back, and repeat this process as I keep walking down the row. Finally, I come across the book I've been looking for and eagerly pick it out, glad to have gotten the last copy.

"What book is that?" a muffled voice comes behind me.

I turn to see Cruise looking over my shoulder, mouth stuffed with fudge. I crack up, covering my mouth with my hand.

"Cruise, how much fudge did you eat?" I say, laughing loudly.

"Uhh, a lot." He grins, the chocolate stuck on his teeth widely visible. "Oops."

"Dummy. Okay, but we're going to find you a book to read," I say, turning back to the shelves and scanning them for something he would be interested in reading.

"No need, Ms. Bibliophile. I got what I wanted."

I turn to see him waving a book in the air, and I reach out to grab it. It's a book of poetry by Maya Angelou, and I look back up at him, raising an eyebrow.

"Maya Angelou, huh?"

His expression becomes calmer, and he nods. "Yup. She's one of my favorite poets. I've got books of Emily Dickinson and Walt Whitman at home, and I've been reading Angelou's work online, but I really wanted a consolidated book of her poems."

I nod, his passion for her poetry making me smile. We walk through a couple more aisles, him picking out some travel books for his mom and me picking some cookbooks for my parents. Ed comes up to us a couple of times, offering us freshly made fudge and laughing when Cruise eagerly takes his samples. After thirty more minutes, we finally make our way to the checkout counter.

"Got something interesting?" Ed says as he quickly works to scan our books.

"Absolutely," Cruise cuts in, clearly hyped up on all the sugar he's eaten.

"Got a full stomach, too," I say, nudging Cruise, and he laughs sheepishly, rubbing the back of his neck.

"I'm glad," Ed says, grinning. He packs our books in a bag and hands them to us. "Have a nice day, you two! Do come back soon."

"Bye!" we say and head out of the store, the sunlight casting its warmth on us.

"Wow, I am full and content and very, very happy right now," Cruise says, bouncing on his toes and looking back at me.

I say, giggling. "The sugar hitting you right about now?"

"Oh, definitely. Maybe I had too much."

"You think? I'm kidding," I say, chuckling when he gives me an affronted look. "I didn't have any fudge, though, so I'm starving. Know any good food spots?"

"Ah, now it is my turn to show off my expertise. Follow me, madam," Cruise says, walking to the left.

I catch up with him, and we walk in comfortable silence, enjoying the quiet that has settled on downtown now that the lunch rush has ended. He leads me to a quaint, light yellow restaurant, and as we enter, the smell of spices hits me.

"Oh, yum," I say, breathing in deeply. "I'm already intrigued."

"Do you like ramen?" Cruise asks as he looks up at the menu.

"Oh, yes. You order for me, though; I trust your knowledge."

Cruise shoots me a thumbs up and walks to the cashier, greeting her with a smile. He must come here a lot, as most of the employees make conversation with him, and he chatters back excitedly to them. I take a seat at one of the small tables near the entrance, looking out of the window at the few people passing by. I pull my book out and read it as I wait for Cruise to come back. I'm soon immersed in my book, and I start when Cruise sets our tray down with a clatter.

"Oh, sorry, I didn't mean to startle you," he says apologetically.

"No, no, don't worry about it," I say, but immediately direct my attention to the masterpieces in front of me. "Oh. my. gosh. This looks like heaven."

"It literally is," Cruise says enthusiastically, handing me a pair of chopsticks.

I take them and take the bowl he hands me as well.

"My parents are huge fans of ramen, and we discovered this place a couple of months ago. We've come here a gazillion times since then."

"I see why. This place is beautiful."

I unwrap my chopsticks and use them to pick up the noodles and vegetables in the rich broth and blow on them to cool them down. I then place them in my mouth and drink a spoon of the broth right after.

"Ohhh," I moan, frantically scooping more of the broth into my mouth as flavor explodes in every corner of my mouth.

"Right?" Cruise says, grinning, as he takes his own bite.

"That is absolutely delicious," I say, mouth full. "I don't think I've ever had ramen as good as this. This is literally amazing."

"It seriously is."

We lapse into silence as we continue eating, too hungry and overcome with deliciousness to stop. A few minutes later, our bowls are empty, their contents filling our bellies, leaving us satisfied and full.

"That was the best meal I've had in a while," I say, my hand on my full stomach.

Cruise nods, agreeing with me. "This place never misses. It's one of those safe food spots."

"Agreed. I will be coming here with my parents very soon. You've just unleashed a whole new age of spending-money-on-food for me," I say, sitting up straight.

Cruise laughs. "I'm glad."

I grin at him, and he smiles back. He gets up to drop our dishes in one of the cleaning boxes, saying he'll be right back. My eyes linger on him as he walks. Today was one of the best days I've had in a really long time, and I'm pleasantly surprised that it was with Cruise. He continues to surpass every previous notion I've had about him, and I'm secretly glad he does. I'm growing to enjoy his company more and more. There's one thing that lingers in my mind, however, and that's Silke's experience with him. Since I've seen the accounts and witnessed their feud first-hand, I know that it isn't a lie that Silke is feeding me.

"So," I start as he takes a seat.

He raises his eyebrows and leans back, folding his arms.

"Uh-oh," he says. "That doesn't sound very good."

"No, nothing too serious. Just a general question." I lean forward, placing my head in my hands.

"Is this about what happened between Silke and me?" he asks, an understanding look coming over his face.

"Yes," I say, surprised that he was able to figure it out.

He nods, leaning back. "What do you know?"

I proceed to narrate the tale that Silke told me, and Cruise listens intently, his eyes narrowing as I continue. When I mention the past, about the stalker accounts, he lets out a laugh and shakes his head.

"Wow," he says, a tinge of hurt in his voice as I finish the story. He shakes his head, looking down at his hands, which are clasped tightly on the table. "I didn't realize that she had twisted the story that much."

"What actually happened?" I gently ask. "I'll be honest, Silke's experience with you has definitely been a red flag for me. I wasn't sure whether you were actually like that because she was pretty convincing in her narration."

"Wait, wait, Sanah," Cruise says, leaning forward and placing a hand on mine, a slight look of sadness on his face. "I'm not like that. Not at all. I would never do something like that."

"And I believe you," I say, squeezing his hand and letting go of it, leaning back in my seat. "As I said before, I judge people based on what I see of them, and I'm finding it harder and harder to believe that you actually did that."

Cruise leans back again as well and takes a deep breath. "Look, it's really difficult for me to talk about this just because it was such a dark time in my life. It really, truly destroyed my mental health."

"And you don't have to say anything about it if you don't want to," I say gently. "However, you can trust me. I know that I'm in that friend group, but as you can tell from the events of yesterday, I'm not really involved with any of them, nor am I particularly fond of them. I really value our friendship, and I want you to feel like you can tell me anything because you can. Honestly."

Cruise looks at me for a few seconds, observing my face. I see the debate raging in his head: it's reflected in his stormy, confused eyes.

Finally, he takes another deep breath, leans forwards, and says, "Alright. Silke and I met for the first time at a summer pool party that her family threw the summer before we entered the sixth grade. She was nice enough at the party, greeting me well and stuff, but she didn't really pay much attention to me. She had her friends there, and I just hung around for an hour before leaving to bike home. I didn't see her for the rest of the summer, and when we entered sixth grade, I only passed her as I walked to class. She didn't notice me, or if she did, she didn't pay any attention to me. The summer before seventh grade—and I know this sounds hopelessly pretentious of me—I went through a huge glow up, and when we got back to school, Silke suddenly began taking a lot more notice of me."

I remember that. In the first few months of seventh grade, all I could remember was everyone saying that they had a crush on Cruise.

"She began to talk to me a lot, and I, unknowing of any other intentions that she may have had, began to hang out with her, presuming that she simply wanted to be my friend. This went on for a few months, and around four months into seventh grade, Silke finally admitted that she liked me. Of course, I didn't like her back. I only thought of her as a friend, and I wanted nothing to do with dating whatsoever. I told her so as nicely as I could. But she became really angry and began pestering me to tell her whether I actually meant that. She seemed determined to somehow push me to start liking her. But I didn't budge. I remember Silke rushing off, fuming. This happened on a Friday, so I didn't see her for two days and didn't really have any contact with her. I remember sending her a text or two just to check in, but she never responded. On Monday, when I opened Instagram, I saw that I was tagged in a post from an account that I wasn't familiar with. When I clicked on it, I saw my name in the bio, along with a series of posts that claimed my hatred for Silke. I was shocked, of course, because I would *never* do such a thing. I also knew that Silke would have seen the account too, and I really wanted to talk to her about it and tell her that I had *nothing* to do with it. The second I got to school, I found Silke and tried to reassure her that this wasn't my doing, but she started crying and rushed off. Even though I hadn't done anything, I felt *horrible*. I hated that someone who I considered to be one of my closest friends was sad. I tried to clear things up with her throughout the week, but she didn't listen. As the week progressed, people began to start drifting away from me because they thought I was mean-spirited and petty for starting that account, even though I knew that I wasn't because *that account wasn't mine*. But I didn't know what to do. When the weekend rolled around, I was immensely grateful for being able to take a break from all the drama that was happening at school. Or so I thought. Over the weekend, I got a text from a family friend that was really close to Silke. I don't think Silke knew that the two of us were friends, or she'd never have texted her. My family friend told me that Silke was the one who had created the account out of spite because Silke claimed that she didn't deserve to be rejected, and this was her way of getting her revenge.

I was completely taken aback because this was so different from the version of Silke I knew, and for a few minutes, I didn't believe it. But when my family friend sent screenshots of texts that Silke had sent her with those exact words, I realized that Silke was serious about getting back at me. Hold on, I probably still have them."

Cruise whips out his phone, taps on it for a couple of seconds, and then hands his phone to me.

"Here, swipe through those pictures. That's the evidence I have."

My hands get sweaty as I read the texts on the screen. Cruise was right: this is all Silke's doing.

"I don't even know what to say," I say, quietly, handing the phone back to Cruise.

I genuinely don't: this is completely shocking to me. After having a story that I'd believed wholeheartedly completely destroyed, I'm not quite sure how to react.

"How do you know this is legit, though?"

"That was the question I had for my family friend when she sent me those as well, and I asked her about it," Cruise says. "Apparently, Silke had reiterated what she'd said in those texts in person to her. But since I still believed Silke to be a close friend of mine, I had my doubts, which was one of the reasons that the first thing I did on Monday was talk to her."

I nod, my stomach twisting upon hearing this news.

"Did you show Silke the screenshots you had when you confronted her? Why didn't you show these to the school? They would have cleared up your name," I say.

"I didn't go into that interaction with the intention of confronting her. I simply wanted to talk to someone I perceived to be a close friend of mine about a rumor that I had heard because I didn't think it was something that was actually true. Also, if I had shown those screenshots to Silke or the school, it would have gotten my family friend in trouble, which I didn't want. I respected her for sending them to me in the first place, and I didn't want to destroy that privacy."

"Makes sense," I say, sighing. "Okay, so what happened when you talked to Silke?"

"Alright. When I saw her, I vaguely mentioned this rumor that I'd heard about her starting that account about me, and I fully expected her to say that it was just that: a rumor. But instead, she gave me an incredibly cold smile and just said, 'In the future, don't mess with me. The worst is yet to come.' She walked off, and I remember just standing there, too stunned to say a thing. Silke was right: the next few weeks turned out to be some of the worst ones I'd ever had. As Silke went around 'clearing her name' or telling people that my supposed actions were a byproduct of my jealousy, I began to lose my friends and felt the general school population get increasingly distant from me. Everywhere I went, I could feel the cold eyes of people boring into my back and hear their hushed, disgusted whispers about my horrible personality. My reputation had completely deteriorated, along with my mental health. After a few months, Silke must've thought that enough damage was done because the Instagram account disappeared, and she stopped talking about me. From what I know, she told people I took it down because I was getting really concerned about my reputation, which was another lie that further ruined what people thought of me. But even though Silke stopped, I've yet to recover from the social impacts of a series of lies about something that I *didn't even do*."

Cruise finishes his story and wipes his eyes.

"Those were some of the worst few months of my life, and Silke was the sole cause of it. I guess I could have told her I wasn't interested in a nicer way, but I don't think I deserved to be hurt *that* badly for saying no. I also knew that all of her friends were involved in her pretense, which is why I was initially so wary of you. I didn't want to talk to you directly because I was really scared that anything I did would be fuel for you to start even more rumors. I couldn't even look in your direction because I was beyond terrified of having my happiness destroyed."

My mouth is wide open. Of course, the rest of my friends knew about the account. It's just another example of how they would pick Silke over anything, regardless of the consequences.

I shake my head, swallowing the lump that has formed in my stomach. "No, Cruise, gosh. I would never have supported something like that. I'm not usually that involved in the group. I didn't even know that she was the one behind the account. I just knew what was happening. I promise I would *never* do something like that."

"And I believe you," Cruise says, nodding. "You aren't like the rest of them."

"Indeed. But seriously, Cruise, I can't even believe this. It was totally different from what I was told happened." I scoff, shaking my head, anger filling me as I think about Silke's lies. "I didn't even stop to think that Silke could have been making things up. I promise you, though, I wasn't involved in any of it. I wouldn't have forgiven myself if I had allowed myself to do something that terrible to someone."

"Yeah, well, it's a small bit of relief," he says, shrugging and picking at the napkin in front of him. "Anyways. That's my side of the story. The *real* side. Whether you consider it that or not," he mumbles at the end.

"Cruise," I say, saddened.

I'm speechless after what he's told me. It just proves how toxic Silke and the rest of them are. Not just to me but to everyone else. It also proves to me that Cruise is someone that I can't lose. He's kind, genuine, and one of the closest friends I've ever had, even though I've just started talking to him. Coming to my house on a Saturday afternoon to hang out with me and do something that *I* want? I've never had that happen. This person is important to me and someone that I need to keep in my life.

"Yeah, so it did suck," he says, rubbing his head. "It's also why I've decided to go to high school outside of this area."

My heart plummets to the ground when I hear that. *What?*

"You're moving?" I ask, my voice shaking ever so slightly.

"Yeah. I've been applying to a bunch of private high schools in Massachusetts, which is where the majority of my family lives. I'd love a fresh start for high school. Plus, some of the schools are really, really good, so I'd be getting an incredible education as well. If I get in, then I'll leave pretty soon so that I can adjust to life there before the stress of academics starts to kick in."

"Ah, that makes sense," I say, suddenly feeling really sad.

I finally felt like I had a true friend, and now he's leaving, and it hits me that even though I'll have Silke and the group's company, I won't really have *friends*. I'll have company. In reality, I'll be alone—a chilling thought that sends shivers down my spine.

But before I begin to think about my own problems, I need to address what Cruise told me.

I look at Cruise's downcast face and gently take his hand. He looks at me, a small, sad smile coming on his face.

"Look, Cruise, I just want to say that I'm not and will never be like that. I'm so sorry for what happened to you because it never should have happened. I hope that you never have to go through anything like that ever again." I squeeze his hand, and this time, keep holding it. "As for me, I promise that I'm not like them and that I will never do anything like that to you. You're already one of the closest friends I've had in a while, and I hope you can grow to trust me on that."

Cruise smiles a little wider and places his other hand on top of mine. "I'm already starting to. In the time remaining before I leave, I'd really love to get to know you more, Sanah. I hope you'd like to too."

We stay like that for a while, and my mind races with the task I've assigned myself. I need to remain friends with Cruise. But I also need to figure out what this story means for my "friendship" with the rest of the group, especially after Cruise moves away. Going off of the events of the sleepover and what Cruise has just told me, it's not just Silke that's the problem: the whole group is confusing. They give up their own opinions to support Silke, and while that isn't right, I've done the same. I know how hard it is to stop listening to her, which is why I don't trust that the rest of the group will have a change of heart toward me. I guess I enjoy the little traditions they do bother to involve me in—having sleepovers and stuff. But is it worth sticking with them if I feel left out and know I'm not really a part of the group? I'm worried about being alone again, especially after what happened last time. But is being in this unappreciative, hurtful group setting really a better option? Should I spend my time with mediocre company when I could be looking out for other quality people?

Do I choose eventual loneliness over having people around me, even if they aren't the best?

I don't know.

CHAPTER ELEVEN

★ ★ ★

A few hours later, I'm back home, sitting on my bed, trying to figure this whole mess out. The lights are dimmed, and I'm under my poofy, blue comfort robe, the one I always wear when I'm trying to figure something out. This time, it's the answer to the following question: do I choose eventual loneliness or … that group? I honestly don't want to answer that question, so I guess my best option is to stay friends with both groups. But how on earth do I do that without my friends blowing up?

I go over to my desk and grab a notebook and a pen. I flip it open to a blank page and title it *Grand master plan for being friends with groups that are mortal enemies.*

You are so extra, the voice inside my head says, and I shush it down. *Let me be extra in peace,* I shoot back.

I sit down again and begin to write out exactly what needs to be done to make this plan a success, and time begins to slip away from me. I scratch out a lot of the things I've written and re-write them over and over and over. The plan needs to be perfect, but it's taking a ridiculous amount of time. I continue to work on it until I'm finally stuck, and the solution to the hindrance is one that I was dreading.

I need to let Cruise in on my plan.

This poses a problem. While Cruise and I are close, I'm not sure if we're close enough for me to ask him to do something like this. What if he's offended that I don't want to be public with our friendship, even though he will understand the reason behind it? But there really is no other way for this to work. He'll keep approaching me at school if I don't tell him, and if I constantly ignore him, he'll get annoyed and possibly stop being friends with me.

"Here's hoping that he cares enough about me, too," I sigh, leaning back on my bed frame.

There really is no other way for this plan to work, so I'm just going to have to shoot my shot and hope for the best. So, I grab my phone and dial his number. Each time the tone rings, my stress jumps up a level, and just when I think I've reached peak anxiety, he picks up.

"Couldn't get enough of me, huh?" I hear him say, and I roll my eyes.

"Oh, please. This was a butt-dial," I respond.

"Ah, I see. Okay, so I'll be hanging up now, then."

"No! No, wait, I was joking, you rat," I say frantically, and I hear a laugh from the other side.

"Ah, so we've resorted to name-calling now. No worries, I can match up just as easily if you want," he says, and I gasp dramatically.

"Ay. Mind it. Don't mess with me."

"Okay, let's not quote Silke, please," he groans, and I burst out laughing.

He starts laughing too, and after a while, says, "Okay, but seriously, I don't think you've called me at 8 PM just to chat. Is everything good?"

I hesitate for a moment, debating how to say everything. Cruise picks up on it.

"Sunny, what's wrong?"

Happiness blooms in my stomach upon hearing him say my nickname, and I build up the confidence to tell him.

"Okay. So. Cruise, as I mentioned earlier, I really enjoy being friends with you. You're already one of the closest friends I have, and I want to continue our friendship."

"Aw," he cuts in, sounding slightly embarrassed but definitely pleased.

"That's really nice of you to say."

"Yeah, of course. However, there's a slight problem, and I think you know what it is," I say, standing up and starting to pace the length of my bedroom.

"Silke," he says, and I hear him take a deep breath. "Yeah, I figured."

"However, I think I've realized that Silke is a total jerk and that I value my friendship with you more than I value mine with her. So—"

"Why?"

I stop walking.

"Why do you value your friendship with her at all? She's been horrible to you, yet you still stick with her. The same thing goes for the rest of your group. You mentioned that they don't include you, but you continue to be friends with them. Why is that?"

I don't know what to say to him because I'm not ready to admit the truth yet. I'm *scared* to admit my reasons. Doing so will bring back a huge flood of awful memories that I know I can't face.

Cruise picks up on the fact that this is a touchy subject for me from the silence that ensues after his question.

"Okay, I take that back. No need to answer that. Continue with what you were saying."

I take a deep, shuddering breath. "I guess it's just difficult for me to talk about the reason. The time before my friendship with the group was beyond difficult. I'm sorry, I don't really want to go that much more into depth."

I know that Cruise wants more of an explanation, but I just can't bring myself to give him one.

"No worries, I don't want to push you to do anything. But go back to your previous point. You were saying that I'm amazing and that I'm obviously the better friend and that Silke is a piece of crap. Continue on, please. I'm loving this."

I scoff, laughing at the same time. "Okay, to quote you, 'this was not an invitation to inflate your ego.'"

"Okay, alright. But seriously, what's going on?"

I take another deep breath, readying myself to explain.

"As you saw earlier, Silke will murder both of us if she knows that I'm still friends with you. But, reasons aside, I can't leave the group. Who, as you can probably guess, doesn't love you. But I also want to stay friends with you. I really, really do. I'd like to make the most of the time we have left before you leave. So, here's my plan. We don't interact other than in history class at school. This means no talking, no hanging out, nothing. *But*, outside of school, we interact as much as we want. It's rather simple, but it'll take some effort to make sure that they don't see us. I know all of their go-to hangout spots, and they're vastly different from the ones I'm presuming that we will enjoy going to, so them seeing us shouldn't be much of a problem." I take a breath in between and then add one last part. "I understand that this is kind of a tall order, and I'm totally alright if you aren't willing to go along with it."

Cruise is silent for a few seconds, and I begin to grow nervous. What if he thinks this plan is way too over-the-top? What if he doesn't want to do it? Am I going to lose the only true friend I've had?

"Okay. Let's do it."

"Oh, really?"

"I'm definitely a bit confused as to why our friendship needs to remain secretive, but I don't want to cause problems for you. Or me. If it has to do with Silke, then there's probably something that will go wrong for us. I'm hesitant, but I'm okay with it."

I'm a bit taken aback. "Really?" I exclaim, confusion clear in my voice.

He laughs. "Yeah, sure. You're definitely important to me as well, and even though we have just started our friendship, I think this can grow to be something really cool."

I'm still shocked, but a wave of happiness flows over me. "Wow, um, okay! That's cool. Thanks. I totally understand the hesitation, but I'll definitely explain my reason for it when I feel comfortable. It isn't a great story, and it does get me down whenever I tell it, so maybe when I'm ready. Thank you for doing this despite your hesitation, though."

"Of course. Please don't feel pressured into saying anything. Go at a pace that's best for you," he says. "Besides, think about it this way: We're as close to starring in a spy movie as we can get. Secret agent vibes."

I start laughing again, shaking my head. "Definitely. Mission hide-us-from-Silke commences now."

I hear the smile in his voice as he responds, "Perfect."

We hang up after that, and I lie down on my bed, excitement and relief flooding over me. *He's staying. We can still be friends.*

However, one little thing lingers at the back of my mind. Another step that needs to be taken to make this plan a success. One that I didn't tell him about: white lies about Cruise to Silke and the rest of the group.

I sit up straight, the thought inciting a new flood of worry. This was the exact reason Cruise was hurt in the first place, and earlier today, I promised him that I wouldn't ever do something like this. However, this has been something I've been thinking about for a while, and it needs to be done in order to make the plan a success. If I talk badly about Cruise every now and then, nobody will suspect anything. Plus, I can keep it in moderation, and he doesn't have to know anything. It's not like Silke is going to go and tell him.

I sigh, running my hands through my hair. *It's fine,* I reassure myself. *This is being done for a good reason. He doesn't need to know anything.*

As I lie back down again, picking up a novel from my bedside, the thoughts keep running through my head.

He will not know anything.

You guys will stay friends.

CHAPTER TWELVE

★ ★ ★

"Sanah, can I sit here? The sun is really nice, and there's a lot of other seats around the table."

I look behind me to see Silke standing with her hands on her hips, smiling thinly at me. The sun was the exact reason that I chose to sit in this spot, but I can't really say no to Silke. Not if I'm trying to stay out of her bad books, especially since I'm doing something that she definitely wouldn't approve of.

"Yeah, for sure," I say, getting up and moving to the end of the table, where the last available seat is.

The girls around me are talking about the picture session they had after Silke's sleepover, and in the spirit of the conversation, I try to seem interested in their pictures while ignoring the sinking feeling of being left out that has gathered in my stomach once more.

"So, Sunny," I hear Silke's voice say.

I look up in surprise, unused to getting direct attention from her. My main friends in the group are Fay and Klyah, and I talk to them most of the time. Silke and I usually only interact in group situations.

"What's going on with Cruise anyways?"

Silke stares right at me, and I feel my stomach turning. I know what I have to do: tell her a lie to throw her off the scent because even if I'm a little bit truthful, she will know.

So, I lie.

I narrate a tale of his shortcomings, how he simply can't do work, how he isn't a good partner. It's just a tad bit more than white lies, but they aren't that bad. They keep me in their favor while keeping me out of trouble.

I feel guilty for lying. But I must do it if I want to save myself.

"Food is ready!" Cruise says, bringing out plates of grilled cheese sandwiches into his living room, their scent filling the room.

"Are grilled cheese sandwiches really all you know how to make?" I say, grinning as I take one and hissing as it scalds me.

"Oy, careful," he exclaims. "Chef Cruise's masterpieces aren't widely available, madam."

"Alright, alright. Shall we try?" I say, raising my sandwich as if to toast.

"We shall," he responds, raising his own and lightly tapping my sandwich.

I take a bite of the sandwich, chewing it, and placing it on the side as I pull out my laptop.

"Okay, so I'm going to work on the essay for English for a while, and then I'll get to work on the project," I say, typing in my password and pulling up my essay.

"Sounds like a plan, madam. I'm going to study for my math test. Here's hoping these equations are kind to me."

I give him a thumbs up and refocus my attention on my essay. I pull out the book the essay is on and begin typing away. Cruise settles down in front of me, staring at his textbook, and we settle into a comfortable silence. Outside, the sun begins to set, and Cruise's automated lights come on. We continue to work, and before we know it, it's close to 7 PM.

Cruise stretches, letting out a grunt of satisfaction. "Okay, I'm done. Those equations were, in fact, not kind to me. But I understand them."

I look up from my essay, smiling. "Nice. Good job."

Cruise puts on a face of offense. "How about upping the admiration? Wow, Cruise, you're so smart, Cruise. See, much better."

"We really need to work on that ego of yours."

Cruise barks out a laugh and comes next to me to swat my arm. "Alright, whatever. I'm gonna go use the bathroom. I'll be right back."

I nod, and as he walks away, I pick my phone out of my backpack, checking my notifications, and I'm surprised to see a huge spam on the group chat. I unlock my phone and scroll up to where the messages start, and my heart drops like a stone.

It's a picture of me wearing a sweater that my *dadi*, or grandmother, knitted for me on my twelfth birthday. It's one of the last gifts I have from her before she passed away. It's purple, red, and blue: not one of the best color combinations, but it's one of my favorite pieces of clothing. I love it, not just because of how pretty it looks to me but also because of the love that was put into making it. But as I scroll through the messages, my stomach twists more and more.

> Continuing our game of dress fails, last victim being Kelly, here we have sunny.

> yikes. that color combo

> not so sunny, sanah

The rest of the messages follow the same pattern, and as a drop of water splatters onto my phone screen, I realize that I'm crying. Surprised, I wipe the tears from my cheeks, but they keep coming. None of them know anything about the history of the sweater. I get that they're playing a game, but the sweater is so incredibly important to me, and they just cast it aside. How dare they? Who gave them the right to say *anything*?

"Sanah?"

I look up and see Cruise standing at the entrance to the dining hall, where we're seated, and see his face immediately twist into one of concern when he notices the tears in my eyes.

"No, Sunny, why are you crying?" he says as he walks over to me and wraps me in a hug.

I can't bring myself to speak. I'm still shaken by their words. So, instead, I turn my head into Cruise's shoulder and cry. And I continue to cry. And Cruise continues to stand there, arms wrapped around me, quiet. We stay like that for a long time until I finally lift my head, sniffling and wiping my tears. Cruise keeps his arms wrapped around me and looks at me, a look of sadness on his face.

"Silke?" he asks, and I nod.

I hand him my phone, and as he reads, I tearfully explain my context. He lets out an angry laugh when I finish and shakes his head, obviously furious.

"This is too much. She has no right to make you this miserable. This is ridiculous. I hate seeing you this sad."

"It's fine," I say quickly.

He looks at me, eyebrows raised.

"They're just playing a game. If I say anything, Silke will get mad, and you know what happens when Silke is mad. Plus, I need to stay friends with them, remember?"

"Even though they make you feel like, like this?" Cruise says, wildly gesturing to me.

His words ring a familiar bell in my mind, and I realize that he's right. But it doesn't matter. I need to stay friends with them.

"Yes," I say, taking a deep breath and wiping the last of my tears off my face. "I do."

Cruise looks at me, long and hard, but says nothing. He runs his hands through his hair and sighs deeply.

"Okay. You know what's best for you." He looks at me again and then suddenly leans in to give me a tight hug. "Be sunnier, Sunny. It doesn't suit you to be rainy."

I let out a sad laugh, all of a sudden incredibly grateful for him. "Oh, gosh," I murmur into his shoulder. "You and your stupid puns."

He leans back and looks me straight in my eyes, placing his hands on my shoulders, his face becoming solemn. "I'm serious, Sanah. You're the last person who should feel or be treated this way."

I smile at him, looking him in his eyes as well. "Thank you, Cruise." And I genuinely mean it.

The butterflies in my stomach are a result of his kindness, though. Nothing more.

He lets go of me and straightens up.

"Let's go," he says, pulling me towards the living room. "It's the long weekend, so let's watch a movie. Your choice. I'll order us some pizza. You deserve to take it easy." He looks over at me, still sitting down. "Get up, Suns. You don't really have a choice here."

I grin, my mood beginning to brighten. "Alright, let's do this."

I shoot my mom a quick text to let her know about my updated plans, and she sends me back a thumbs up, signaling her approval. I walk towards Cruise's living room, my mind surprisingly free of thoughts.

Silke and the rest of them may be horrible. But I can manage them if I have Cruise with me.

CHAPTER THIRTEEN

★ ★ ★

A few hours later, I'm feeling a lot better. Cruise had ordered pizza from my favorite place, and we had started watching a movie, but we got bored after a while and started to play card games. When Cruise's parents came home, they greeted me enthusiastically and joined in to play with us, and we ended up having a lot of fun.

When I get home, I'm exhausted, and I quickly narrate the day's events to my parents (excluding the part about the comments) and get into bed. I check my phone once before putting it away and see a text from Cruise.

Hope you're feeling better :)

I absolutely am. thank you :)

anytime.

★ ★ ★

On Saturday afternoon, my mom drops me off at the quaint little coffee shop near Cruise's house, one of my favorite working spots. I wave goodbye to my mom and walk inside; the sweet smell of coffee, loud whirs of espresso machines, and the crunch of coffee beans as the baristas grind them hitting me—my comfort sounds.

Cruise and I decided to meet to finish up our applications to the private high schools we're applying to. I spot him sitting at a table in the back and walk over to him, knocking on the table to get his attention.

"Hey!" he says excitedly, gesturing to the seat in front of me.

I drop my backpack and walk over to him, ruffling his hair and laughing when he yelps.

"My hair is too precious for you to mess with, brat."

"Ah, the signature name-calling. Which school are you working on essays for?" I say, placing my hands on either side of his chair and looking at his computer screen.

"My favorite one, but these essays will be the death of me," Cruise grumbles.

"Agreed," I say, shaking my head. "We got this, though. I'm going to go get myself a coffee. Be right back."

Cruise nods, still typing away, and I walk over to the cashier and order myself a Caffè Mocha. Not the healthiest, but I always need a sugar and caffeine rush when working on applications. I wait around, watching the barista make my drink, and thank her when she hands it to me with a warm smile.

I walk back to Cruise and sit down, pulling out my computer and opening the tab with my essays on it. We lapse into a comfortable silence, both of us working hard. Once more, the sun begins to set outside, and our coffee cups get emptier and emptier.

"Mind proofreading one of my essays?" I ask Cruise, and he nods, reaching out his hand for my computer.

We exchange, and I begin editing his, making minor grammatical corrections and adding my suggestions.

"This is pretty good, Sunny," Cruise says, sounding impressed.

"Same with yours. These are really good. The connection to music? Awesome."

"Thanks!" I say, smiling. "Alright, that's enough essay writing for today. I'm tired."

"Agreed," Cruise says, stretching. "Wanna talk?"

An amused look comes onto my face. "About what? Yes, I'm down to talk, but you sound serious."

Cruise leans forward, elbows on the table. "You need to dissect what is going on with Silke. The way you felt on Thursday wasn't normal. You were hurt. But you *still* decided to stick with the group. Why?"

I look at him and take a deep breath, looking down at my nearly empty coffee cup. Nobody knows but my family. But Cruise is right. He should know.

"Ok. Here's my story."

He nods and gets up to sit in the chair next to me. That small, comforting gesture pushes me to begin. I swallow hard, lift my coffee cup up and drain the rest of my drink.

"I moved to the U.S. from India just before the start of middle school. Because the school system in the U.S. works differently, I was forced to skip the fifth grade and go straight from fourth grade to sixth grade. Skipping grades when you're that young doesn't seem like much of a big deal, but it was really difficult to deal with those academic struggles while also experiencing *major* culture shock. While I did study advanced curriculum back in India, I still found it really hard to keep up with the classes when I first joined. I remember spending countless late nights at my dining table with my mom or dad, learning the different concepts for each of my classes, desperately trying to catch up to everyone else so that I could stay on track with my academic goals," I say.

I can already feel myself choking up, but Cruise places a hand on mine, silently telling me to go on. So I do.

"That wasn't even the worst part. The loneliness was. I genuinely felt like an alien. It seemed like nobody liked my personality, no matter how much I tried to make friends or gel with the rest of the people here. On the first day of middle school, I tried talking to some people, but everyone seemed to have their own friend groups, and nobody was particularly interested in adding the 'weird one from India' to their own. That's word for word what I heard one girl I spoke with calling me as I walked away. So I sat down on the bleachers in front of the basketball court, eating my apples and reading the book I had brought from home. I'm not saying that I felt sorry for myself in that situation. I'm proud of the way I handled it, but it's just one example of the kind of loneliness I experienced. Every day, it seemed like I'd be in my own solitary bubble while everyone around me had other people to permeate theirs. After countless attempts to befriend people, I began to wonder if there was something fundamentally wrong with me because I was lonely, that I was doing something wrong. Maybe it was the way I dressed. Maybe it was the things I talked about. Maybe I wasn't a likable person in general. I was really miserable. It wasn't completely because I didn't have anyone around me, but more because of what I thought that implied about me because I truly began to believe that I was the problem. That I had some sort of genuine flaw in my personality, something that I couldn't identify and would never be able to fix, which would lead me to continue being alone."

I feel tears welling up in my eyes, but I force them down and continue.

"My self-confidence hit an all-time low, and I found myself crying nearly every single night. My family did everything they could to help me: they spent every spare second they had with me. Their company is something that I will be eternally grateful for, and while I really appreciated it at the time, it sparked another fear in me: what if I'd never be able to find people beyond my family? What if I was so annoying that only my family would be able to stand me? What if my family found me annoying too? I basically fell into spirals of overthinking about my personality, my identity, and the people I did and didn't have around me. This continued all throughout sixth grade, and when the seventh grade started, I found myself alone once again. I physically felt dread pool in my stomach when I realized that I may just have to go through another year alone and in misery. However, when I became friends with Fay and Klyah in math that year and started to hear about Silke and her friend group, I realized that they had the kind of bond that I'd craved. They did everything together: met up before, during, after school, hung out at every free moment they had, and knew every single detail about each other. I wanted that. I *needed* that. I knew that if I could somehow insert myself into the group, I'd have friends that stuck with me no matter what. And so, I slowly began to change myself to better fit them. I took on a fake personality, started doing the same things they were interested in, and basically modeled myself after them. I became really close with Fay and Klyah, and soon, they asked me to sit with them. I was absolutely ecstatic. I finally, *finally* had friends and really good ones too. Things went great for the first couple of weeks. I felt genuinely happy for the first time in a really long time. However, putting on a fake personality required a ton of extra effort from me, and it was a tiring process. I came home from school exhausted every single day. So, I thought that since I was already friends with the girls, they would accept my true personality, and I slowly stopped being that fake version of myself and readopted my old self. But, as they saw more of who I truly was, they didn't like it. I guess they were only looking for some version of me that best suited them. The more I became myself, the less I found myself involved in the group. And the fear that ran through me when I realized that this personal endeavor might leave me drowning in the abyss of loneliness again left me struggling to breathe. I couldn't be natural because I *could not* be lonely. So I switched back to that personality that they liked so that I could stay, and everything was alright again. I've continued that way ever since. I've been able to be a little natural in front of Fay and Klyah, but the moment those characteristics go against what Silke wants or what the general group dynamic is, I'm shot down for it. You saw that a few days ago."

The tears are flowing freely now, and Cruise wraps his arms around me. I put my head down on his shoulder and take a few moments to just cry. I haven't let myself think about that era in an entire year, but as the memories flow back, so do all the repressed emotions. After a few moments, I gather myself, taking in heaving breaths as I attempt to quiet down a bit.

"I know I shouldn't change myself so drastically. But obviously, the person I really am doesn't deserve friendship. I can't go back to being myself because I *can't* be alone, Cruise, I can't. I really just can't. I can't feel that way again because it'll absolutely destroy me. It nearly did the last time, and I barely made it out of that. I don't think I can make it through a second repetition."

I break down at that point, crying so hard that I'm silent. Cruise holds onto me tightly as my tears soak into his shirt. After a few minutes, once I've calmed down a bit, he lets go of me and turns my face toward his.

"Look, Sunny, I have no words for this. I can't even begin to imagine what that felt like, and I'm so, so sorry that you had to go through that. You are incredibly courageous for getting through that, and I have all sorts of respect for you right now." he says, smiling gently at me.

I give him a watery smile back, one that drops off my face instantly.

"But you need to listen to me," he says, his face turning serious. "Sanah, you are one of the most genuine people I've ever met, and I'm not just saying this to say it. Your excitement is contagious, your dedication to your goals is practically unbelievable, and I'm obsessed with your mind and the way you think. I've never felt so connected to a person in my life. Sanah, you are so, so worthy of friendship. You're not allowed to *ever* think otherwise. You deserve the best kind of people, the kind that make your face light up when they walk in the room, the kind that you stay up late talking to because you just don't want to stop, the kind that make you genuinely happy when you think about them. Because, Sunny, you are that person to me, and I know for a fact that you will find other people who think that too."

I melt at Cruise's words. Warmth blooms in my heart, spreading all throughout my body as I look into his eyes.

"I don't mean to make this about myself. But, when I was going through my issues with Silke, I was incredibly lonely for quite a while, too, as most of my friends left me to avoid having their reputations ruined or to avoid having me hurt them as well. It hurt. A lot. I tried doing everything I could in order to be someone that other people liked and not the person that Silke was painting me to be. However, I learned firsthand that trying too hard for people that don't care literally doesn't matter. They don't care. They never will. Changing yourself for people who couldn't give a crap about you doesn't mean that they will start like you: they *still* won't care. From what you described about the sleepover, it definitely seems like the company of your friends is conditional, that they only provide it when you seem to match the person *they* want you to be. But why do you change yourself for *them?* They don't care: let's be completely honest about that. Sanah, who you really are is such a beautiful person. Why are you hiding that for people that don't even deserve the fake version of who you are? For people that don't deserve *you?*"

I take in his words and mull them over. He's right. I guess they don't care, not in the slightest. But I've never even imagined taking that thought seriously. It still fills me with utter dread, but for the first time, I'm considering leaving to be an actual possibility. Although I know it'll take me some effort to muster up the courage to really do it, Cruise's words finally plant the idea in my mind for good.

"Thank you," I say, tightly hugging him.

The concerned look on his face dims as he hugs me back.

"You're my favorite person, Cruise."

"And you're mine, Sunny."

CHAPTER FOURTEEN

★   ★   ★

Upon returning home, I'm exhausted: both emotionally and physically. I plop down on the couch next to my parents, who are scrolling through Netflix, trying to find a movie to watch. My parents recently redid our living room, and I'm still getting used to it. Our old living room was a plain, white painted box, but my parents took it upon themselves to paint one wall a dark blue, install new, white cupboards, and attach a flatscreen TV to the wall, and it looks gorgeous. I dig my toes into the soft carpet, grabbing the remote for the room's lights to dim them.

"Tired?" my dad asks, punching me lightly in the arm.

"Yeah," I say, yawning.

I lean on my dad, and he puts an arm around me. I shut my eyes, blocking out the light coming from the television.

"Do you want to go upstairs to sleep?" my mom asks, and I open my eyes sleepily.

"Yeah, I think I might. I'm honestly really tired. Sorry, you guys, I did want to watch this movie with you."

"No worries, *beta*, rest. Goodnight!" my mom says, and my parents wave at me.

I wave back and start walking towards the stairs when a text I receive makes me stop in my tracks.

wanna get lunch tomorrow? :3

It's from Silke.

I almost drop my phone when I read it. Silke wants to get lunch with me? *Me?*

Even though the breakdown from earlier is fresh in my mind, so are the feelings of desperation for friends. I can't help it. My mind, once again, goes into overdrive. If Silke is reaching out, then maybe there's hope. Maybe she wants to make up for what happened at the sleepover. Maybe she's trying to care about me for who I really am. What if this is a real opportunity? What if I can get them to care about me and really find those friends? I think it's worth giving her one final try before I make my decision about what to really do.

"Hey, Mama? Papa?" I say, and my parents turn to look at me. "Silke is asking if I want to get lunch tomorrow. Can I go?"

"Sure. Do you really want to, though?" my mom asks, her eyebrows raised.

I hesitate, understanding the reason behind her question. On top of that, my conversation with Cruise from earlier floats through my mind again. However, although his points are valid, I don't think I'm quite ready to completely give her up yet. Silke and I have been friends for a while, and maybe I can use this lunch to clarify things with her and figure out what's really going on.

"I think I do. It'll be nice to talk to her separately," I say slowly, and my mom nods again.

She looks unsatisfied with my answer but agrees to let me go nonetheless. I trudge up the stairs, the moment of excitement over and exhaustion flooding over me once again. I flop onto my bed, stretching, and then turn over onto my side and close my eyes. I'm not sure how I feel about tomorrow. I'm definitely not excited, but I think it'll be a good opportunity for me to make it seem like I'm close to her so that she doesn't even think of the possibility that I may be friends with Cruise.

Hopefully, she doesn't have any nefarious plans for me.

The next day, I wait for Silke at the fancy burger place downtown. I love the burgers; they're pretty popular. The restaurant is bustling with activity, its glass tables packed with people and food. The restaurant has a modern feel to it, with an expansive bar on the far end of the room and a dark, wooden interior. From the kitchen comes the faint sound of burger patties frying on the grill and the familiar smell of comfort, American food. I bounce on the tops of my white converse, which I paired with a red and white crop top and a simple pair of jeans. My hair hangs free over my shoulders, and I have a simple gold bracelet on. I glance at my phone, checking the time. Silke is already fifteen minutes late, and although I'm a usually patient person, I tap my finger on the back of my phone impatiently.

I decide to go get us a seat, asking the restaurant host about a table for two. She leads me to a seat outside on the sidewalk, and I ask for water and a small bowl of salad as an appetizer. The rest of the patio seats under the white, windowed tent are full, and I start scrolling through my phone as I wait. It's past noon, and I'm starving. I munch on the salad, staring at my phone as the time inches closer and closer to 12:30, thirty minutes past when we were supposed to meet. Just when I'm about to call Silke, I hear her rush up.

"Hey, I'm so sorry for making you wait," she says, an apologetic look on her face. "My mom and I got into an argument, and it totally slipped my mind to text you about it. You look really pretty!"

She bends down and gives me a hug before sitting down in her seat. I feel a bit better now that she's apologized, and we jump into an animated conversation about track tryouts. We keep chatting all throughout lunch, and when we've finished our meals, I'm feeling surprisingly comfortable with her. Although Cruise's words echo in my mind, I put them aside for a few moments, enjoying the time I'm spending with her.

"Alright, so. Fill me in because we haven't talked about this yet. What's it like working with Cruise?"

My guard instantly goes up. I know that Silke will expect me to say only bad things about Cruise because she believes that we aren't close whatsoever, and that's the last thing I want to do. The thing that ruined Cruise was lies about his personality, and I don't want to be the one saying those to Silke. However, considering the way our conversation has gone today, perhaps there's some room for a closer friendship to grow? I know that Cruise explained the importance of surrounding myself with quality people, but I'm just not ready to let go of them yet, especially now that there might be a chance for us to become closer. Maybe if I say just a *few* white lies about Cruise, that process may start. And so, I take a deep breath and begin.

"Yeah, he isn't much better. The other day, we were working on our projects as usual, right? We were at the library, and one of his friends came up and started talking to him. He just totally left the work and immediately started talking to his friend. He never even came back to work on it and left it all for me. I got so mad. It's like he only cares about himself."

Alright, so maybe it was a bit more than a white lie. But from the way Silke's demeanor changes, from the way she leans in, her eyes bright and engaged, I know that my words have paved a path to get closer to her.

"Sounds like him," Silke says, rolling her eyes. "He never cares at all. He's like, quite possibly, one of the dumbest people I've met."

This is a blatant lie, and I almost laugh out loud at this. But this charade seems to be working, and giddy with excitement at having the opportunity to cement my standing with her and in the group, I take it to the next level.

"I know. You know, he's been talking about you to me."

"He what?" Silke exclaims, obviously shocked.

She leans in even closer, bewildered but obviously enjoying the attention that she is supposedly getting from him.

"Explain, *now*. What did that little jerk say?"

"Yeah, Sanah, what did that little jerk say?"

My heart drops. I freeze, my blood turning ice cold. The voice behind me is familiar, one that I would recognize anywhere. The sour expression that comes onto Silke's face further reaffirms who I think the voice belongs to. Slowly, I turn around and see Cruise standing there.

And my heart breaks.

His face has contorted into a pained look, so raw that it floods through me, causing every inch of my body to splinter into a thousand pieces. His eyes aren't teary, but the stony look behind them reveals how guarded he's become. The stony look that I was able to tear down has returned. And that slams into me so hard that I push away from the table immediately, my chair scratching on the ground and the table rattling.

"C-Cruise," I stammer, unable to form words.

How much has he heard?

"Please, do go on and explain, Sanah," he says, his voice dangerously low, his arms seemingly crossed normally, but the popping veins in his hands show just how tight he's clenching his fingers together.

"Oh, stop overreacting," Silke says, putting a hand over my shoulder. "You've been talking about me, huh? I guess you just can't get over me. You're just the same obsessed, creepy loser you were before. And now you've roped Sanah into it too. Well, she knows the truth about you. Right, Sanah?" Silke looks over at me.

My mind is racing, the choice I must make becoming clearer by the moment. Do I nod, hurt someone I'm extremely close with, and become the person I told Cruise I wasn't? Or do I side with Cruise and ruin my friendship with this group?

Do I choose company or loneliness?

Do I choose Silke or Cruise?

"Sanah?" I heard Cruise's voice say.

It comes out low and harsh but trembles ever so slightly, enough for me to understand how much he wants this to be false. *None of this is true,* I think to myself, begging Cruise to somehow understand. I shouldn't nod. I shouldn't take the side of a group that has hurt me more than I've ever been hurt before, and I shouldn't abandon someone who has made me the happiest I've been in a while.

So,

I nod.

Because I can't lose them. Not yet. I'm not ready.

Because I'm terrified of being alone once he leaves. I can't do it.

Because i can't go through that again. i can't

i cant i really cant i wont be miserable again i wont spiral again and again and i wont let myself hate myself i cant hate myself i hate myself for doing this i cant do it anymore

I nod.

Cruise's face becomes a mask, but his eyes give it all away. The calm ocean in his eyes turns stormy as the waves get higher and higher, threatening to drown me, no, I'm already drowning.

Cruise scoffs, looking down at his feet and saying, "Okay."

And then he walks away.

"Good riddance," I hear Silke say, but my mind is blank.

I can't seem to process anything. *I lost him, I lost him, and I lost him.* Cruise gets farther and farther away from me. *No, why are you leaving? Don't leave me, please, please I can't be alone,* and I just

stare.

I feel Silke pull on my sleeve, ask me why I'm being weird, why I'm out of it because I'm so out of it because I'm so sad, I'm so so so sad.

And then, everything clears. I fall back into reality.

"Silke, shoot, what if he totally flakes on the project because of this?" I say, moving backward in the direction that Cruise went. "I think we should hang out another day. I don't want to get a B or C because of his … his stupidity." I force the words out, letting their sour taste coat my mouth. Silke, thankfully, seems understanding and nods.

"Yeah, you go deal with that loser. I'll call someone else to hang out. Good luck."

The moment she finishes, I'm speedwalking in the direction that Cruise left. I see him turn the corner and break into a run, scared that I'm going to lose him. I dash past restaurants and stores, places that just a few weeks ago, we had made plans to come to. The plans that will never be carried out.

"Cruise!" I shout as I turn the corner and spot him.

He doesn't turn around. I increase my speed, my running practice coming in handy, and I finally catch up to him. He's turned into an empty residential street, and as we keep moving forward, the noise from the downtown setting begins to fade away. I slow my pace and try to catch my breath.

"Cruise, please," I say, placing a hand on his arm, but I'm startled back when he violently moves away.

"Don't," he says, his voice low and shuddering.

It pains me to hear how hurt he sounds.

"Cruise, please; I'm sorry—"

"Don't say you're sorry," he says, whipping around to look at me, anger pulsing through his eyes. "You aren't sorry. You really would do anything to get in their favor, wouldn't you?"

"Cruise, no, I didn't mean it," I say, my voice breaking.

The tears have begun to fill in my eyes, and I'm trying hard not to let them spill over.

He laughs, the sound piercing through the air. "You didn't mean it? Sure, Sanah. Let's say that you didn't. But you still put down someone that you were *presumably* really close to, someone that thought of you as their closest companion, just to get in her favor. You said that we would fake a friendship, but you never mentioned that *you* were going to be fake too. You just did *exactly* what Silke did to me."

The comparison to Silke hits me like a truck, and I feel myself take a step back. I feel my tears fall faster and faster. He suddenly moves closer, gripping my shoulders with his hands. When I look up, surprised, I see tears shining in his eyes.

"Sanah, you did the one thing I told you broke me before. Rumors. Everything you said was false and had the potential to make last year repeat again. You *know* how much that would hurt me. But you don't care, do you? You're just Silke's little puppy dog, doing anything, *anything*, to get in her favor. It's sickening."

I'm left speechless, not just at his words but at their accuracy. He's hit me exactly where it hurts.

"Cruise, please, just let me explain," I start, and he shakes his head, looking back at me, his face stony once more.

"No, Sanah. There's nothing to explain anymore." He walks closer again. "Has this been going on since we started being friends? Have you been feeding your friends lies since we came up with that plan?"

My silence tells him everything, and he steps backward again, a look of utter disbelief on his face. "Wow. I can't, I, wow."

"Cruise, I'm sorry. I'm so, so sorry."

He shakes his head, a look of calm determination coming onto his face. "No, Sanah. I think I'm done here. If you don't value me enough to do something that I practically begged you not to do, if my best friend can't do that for me, then I don't want that person in my life. I'm done. We're done."

My heart breaks.

No. He can't leave me. I can't lose him. Panicked, I beg him to stay: pleading, crying, and apologizing over and over, but he shakes his head.

"The damage is done. Goodbye."

And with those words, the most important person in my life turns around and walks away—walks away from me—walks right out of my life.

He was leaving already, but knowing it was for good this time hurts even more.

And

    I

        break

I don't even care about what the people around me think: they've judged me enough based on the other things they just saw.

I collapse onto the ground, tears streaming down my face, sobbing.

My mind grieving for the person I've lost.

My brain cursing me for the mistake I've made.

My heart broken beyond repair.

CHAPTER FIFTEEN

★   ★   ★

I text Silke that I'm leaving early, dazed and completely out of it. I need time to calm down, to digest what has just happened. I pick myself up from the ground and slowly begin to walk home instead. I pull out my phone and call Cruise over and over and over. I text him, asking if I can explain, if we can talk.

No response.

My eyes begin to fill up once again, and I take a shuddering breath. *Shoot, Sanah,* I think. *You complete, utter, idiot. You ruined it; you ruined something perfect. What have you done?*

When I finally get home, I sit on my front steps for a bit, unwilling to go inside. I check my phone once more but still see nothing from him. I know he's furious, and I hate it.

"Sun?" I hear a voice say from behind me, and I turn to see my mom.

Her face becomes immediately concerned when she sees my tear-streaked face, and she sits down next to me.

"What's wrong? What happened?"

Voice breaking, I narrate what happened, and her face drops more and more as I do.

"Sunny, come on," she says, the disappointment in her voice clear enough to make me cry even harder.

"I made a mistake, I know," I say, my voice shaking. "I just don't know what to do to fix it."

My mom looks at me, the tears running down my cheeks and the distraught look on my face, for a moment before letting out a breath and rubbing my back.

"Look, Sunny, considering what you said about the true series of events that happened between Silke and Cruise, I can't tell you that what you did is alright because it's not," my mom says, sighing. "I understand that you're scared of being alone, but that's a better option than turning yourself into a total jerk to suck up to someone who really doesn't care about you or anyone else. I know you're a loyal person, but your loyalty should be towards the *right* type of people."

I hold my tears back. I always prioritized company over loneliness but never really understood what having mediocre people around me could lead to. Cruise was the one good friend I had, someone I could turn to when I got tired of my own group. But after today, after my selfish words, my "friends" are all I have left. Cruise is gone, and I am alone.

"Look, in this case, I think you should give Cruise some time to calm down," my mom continues. "Knowing you, I'm sure that you'll be able to talk to him about your feelings and apologize, but you should give him some time right now."

My heart sinks. I don't want to have to spend time without him. I need to be able to talk to him.

"Okay," I say unwillingly.

It's something I don't want to have to do at all. But I know I must.

My mom finally smiles at me and squeezes my shoulder.

"Everyone makes mistakes, Sun. Don't worry too much. I know this will be hard, but you can get through this." She stands up, dusts off his pants, and asks me if I'm coming inside, her face transformed into a look of concern.

"In a bit," I say.

She nods and goes back inside. I remain sitting on the steps, letting my mind calm down. My mom is right, but I don't want to just stop trying. I pull out my phone and tell myself to send just one last text, and when I do, I get up and go inside. I head up the stairs and into my room and fall onto my bed, too exhausted to piece my broken self together.

The next day, my heart is beating out of my chest as I walk into history. I'm terrified to face him, to see him. But I'm also beyond eager. Seeing him face to face gives me a chance to explain myself. A chance that I desperately need.

When I enter, I see most students sitting with their partners, chatting lightly before they begin work on their projects. The low murmur of conversation suddenly seems ominous. My heart drops for a moment but then lifts a second later as I realize that this forces conversation between me and Cruise to happen.

I drop into my seat, pulling out my laptop and pretending to be focused on my work as I wait for Cruise to walk in. After a few minutes of waiting, he does, and his face drops instantly when he realizes that we're working in our partnerships today. I see him look around for me, and when he spots me, he grudgingly walks over and sits in the seat in front of me. He doesn't say a word. My mind races, trying to figure out what to say to him.

"Hi," I say softly, and he doesn't respond. I swallow hard and decide to push once more. "Um, so, should we just work on the slides?"

"You work on your essay; I'll work on mine," Cruise says, his voice harsh and gritty.

My heart sinks a little more, but I think that this is a good time to bring up this conversation.

"Cruise, please," I whisper, leaning in. "Please, can we talk?"

"Sanah, there's nothing to talk about," Cruise says, finally turning to look at me and glaring at me.

It makes me shrivel back.

"Do your own work. I don't want to talk to you."

He turns back around and begins typing on his laptop, ignoring me. I stare at the back of his head, my mind whirling. This isn't happening anytime soon, which is a problem, considering that he's leaving as soon as he gets an acceptance from a school, and decision season is just around the corner. I need to make this right *before* he leaves: I just don't know how.

We continue to work in silence for the rest of the period as the chatter of all the other groups surrounds us, and when the bell rings, Cruise immediately gets up and leaves without so much as a second glance back at me. I get up slowly after him and walk out, dejected. The happy chaos outside makes me want to yell. I don't know what to do. I'm stuck. I know I should wait, but if he's showing this much hatred toward me, is he really going to change his opinions? Yeah, I have my other group of friends, but do I really care anymore?

When I reach the veranda, I'm the first one there, and I wait there for the rest of my group. And I wait. And wait. And continue waiting. About twenty minutes into lunch, I'm thoroughly confused about where everyone is. The familiar, lonely feeling begins to creep up on me, and I'm terrified. *No, I* think. *I can't be alone.* I can't be alone. It grips me by the throat, and I have to claw it off, trying desperately not to let it consume me. I get up and sling my backpack on so I can walk around and try not to feel like this. Just when I'm about to leave, I spot the group walking towards me.

"You guys, where were you?" I say, hating how panicked my voice sounds.

"In Silke's English class. Didn't you get the text? It's on the Instagram group chat." Delhi says.

"What Instagram group chat?"

Her face freezes as she realizes she's revealed something that she shouldn't. She stutters for a few moments and then just looks away. Dread begins to pool in my stomach. *So they have a separate group chat,* I think. I look at Fay and Klyah, who aren't looking at me, their eyes trained on the ground.

And suddenly, I'm angry. No, I'm *furious.* If they aren't treating me the right way, in the way a friend *should* be treated, then why am I putting in so much effort? I threw away someone extremely important to me just so that I remain friends with them, but am I really friends with them if they're treating me this way? While I did feel panicked when I was alone just now, it's not like I missed my friends because I wanted their company. I only "missed" them because I couldn't stand being lonely. Is that reason enough to stay?

And finally, the realization dawns on me. I'd rather be alone than miserable because there's absolutely no point in surrounding myself with people who don't care. And if I'm alone, it doesn't mean there's something wrong with me: it just means I haven't found the people who appreciate me for who I truly am. I *choose* to be alone because I'd rather do that than force myself into an environment where not only am I not wanted, but I honestly don't want to be.

As for this group, they *don't* care. None of them, not even Fay or Klyah. So why do I continue to change myself to fit in with them? Why do I put myself through this?

Holding onto them isn't doing me any good. Throwing away Cruise for them isn't doing me any good. Throwing *myself* away for them isn't doing me any good, and I refuse to lose who I really am for people who couldn't care less.

I'm done.

This may mean that I'm alone, but that's fine.

At least I'm alone, myself, and happy.

CHAPTER SIXTEEN

★　★　★

I follow my mom's advice and let a week of awkward, stilted interactions with Cruise pass. But when I've determined that the time is right, I decide to take action.

My heart pounds as I walk up Cruise's driveway—beating so hard that I'm scared it'll jump right out. "Nervous" isn't even the right word to describe how I'm feeling right now: I've long passed that. I'm terrified. I'm terrified that Cruise will never forgive me—that I'll lose the best friend I've ever made in my life. But this is the only way to get him back. I need to talk to him.

I take a deep breath before I knock firmly on his door three times. It doesn't have one of those peepholes, so he won't know who it is until he opens it. A benefit for me. I hear him coming down the stairs, my heart beating harder with every footstep I hear. When he comes to the door, he stops for a moment. My heart sinks, terrified that he somehow magically knows that it's me at the door. But then, he opens it.

The disgusted look that comes onto his face hits me like a ton of bricks. It hurts so, so much to see him look at me that way. He immediately begins to close the door, but I stick my hand out to stop him.

"Cruise. Please."

I hate how my voice comes out, pleading and cracking, about to rip from the pain. However, something about it makes Cruise stop pushing on the door and pull it back open. He stares straight into my eyes, and I force myself not to shudder from the fury radiating from him. But then, he pulls the door open wider and turns around to walk away. A silent invitation.

I scramble inside before he changes his mind, quietly shutting the door. Cruise doesn't stop walking. I follow him inside, all the way to his living room, and remain standing at the entrance even though he sits down on his couch.

"What do you want, Sanah?"

Just when I thought my heart couldn't break anymore, it does. He sounds miserable. Like he's grappled with the idea of this interaction so much that he can't imagine that it's actually happening, but now that it really is, he doesn't know how to react. I swallow hard, trying to remove the lump in my throat. We need to have this conversation. I just hope it happens in the way I want it to.

"Cruise, please, please hear me out," I say, my voice trembling. "I'm sorry, I'm so sorry. I know that must mean nothing to you right now, but I really am. There's a lot, like, an insane amount of regret for what I did and how things turned out between us. Every single day, I realize I threw away one of the most genuine friendships I ever had, that I threw away someone I really, truly enjoyed being around. It physically hurts me to think about you—like, my heart genuinely hurts, and I'm always hurting because I'm always thinking of you, even though you may not be thinking about me. I can't even begin to explain how much I regret hurting you, the person that literally means everything to me."

I take a deep breath and wipe off the tears that have begun to fall down my cheeks. Cruise's face remains stony. It makes my heart sink even deeper, but I continue to talk anyway.

"Look, simply put, I miss talking to you, I miss our friendship, I miss everything about you. You were and still are my comfort person, regardless of whether you consider me to be the same for you. I'll never be sorry enough for how I made you feel, but just know that I regret it every single day, at every single freaking moment. I needed to lose you to really realize how important you are to me, and even though that sounds horrible, I understand now. Cruise, you are the most amazing person I've ever befriended. Who would give up their entire Saturday to hang out with me at a bookstore with a mere six hours of previous knowledge about how I feel? Who would support every decision that I ever make, no matter the impact on them? Nobody. Except you."

He stares at me, his eyes getting hollower by the second. I continue.

"There are some events that change you instantly, without any effort at all, and this has been one of them. I've taken everything we talked about in our last conversation and truly worked to make them true. I'm leaving Silke and the rest of that group behind because I'm done changing myself to fit in with a group of people that don't care about me. And if that means that I'll be alone, then so be it. At least I'll be happy."

I take a deep breath and finish, my voice shaky.

"I'm a firm believer in giving people second chances, especially if they're willing to be open and honest about accepting their mistakes. And that's what I'm doing here: accepting every single mistake I've made in this situation. I was a horrible, horrible friend, a horrible person, and I can't say sorry enough for it. I understand if there's hesitation from you because if I were in your place, I would absolutely feel it too. However, all I'm asking is for another chance for our friendship. Losing you has been one of the hardest things I've had to go through. I can live without your friendship, but I don't want to, Cruise, because it was one of the purest things I've ever had. You're my person, and you're always going to be my person, regardless of what happens between us. So, please, Cruise, please. Please be willing to give our friendship another shot."

I'm practically sobbing as I finish, and Cruise just

stares at me.

And he keeps staring as I cry harder

and harder

and harder.

Unmoving. Eyes cold. Face emotionless.

So, so distant.

I control myself and somehow force my eyes up to his. Our eyes lock, and we just

stare.

And stare

and stare

and stare.

And just when I can't take it anymore, just when the tears have begun to fall down my cheeks once more, Cruise looks down at his hands, sighing, slumping forward. I hold my breath, anticipation filling my entire body. When he looks at me, I almost fall with relief when I see that, although the rest of his body is rigid, his eyes have softened. He stands up and closes the wide, gaping distance between us, and stands directly in front of me, staring at his feet. I don't speak. He stands there for a few moments, and I dare to lift a hand and place it gently on his arm. This time, he doesn't shrug away. Instead, he holds onto it and pulls me into a hug.

I'm so surprised that I let out a small cry of confusion and feel him laugh into my shoulder when I do. We stand there for a few moments, relief and the unanticipated feeling of exhaustion filling me. *Did I get him back? Did I do it?*

"Oh, Sunny," I hear Cruise say, and he leans back to look me straight in the eye, a sad smile on his face.

I try to put a smile on my own, but my eyes fill when I do, the tears spilling over. Gently, he puts his hand on my cheek and wipes them off with his thumb. My heart is going at a million miles an hour, and my brain is thoroughly confused. My heart, however, is pleasantly happy. Giddy happy.

"I'm leaving on Saturday."

My paradise breaks into a thousand pieces, black clouds raining so so so hard onto me, drenching me with news that i wish i could claw out of my ear because no no no

 I'm moving, each raindrop paints as it splatters onto the ground

  the same way my heart has broken open when it hit the ground along with me because i've collapsed, unable to comprehend that he's gone.

"Wh-What?" I stutter, stumbling back.

No. No. Is this because of me? Did I push him to leave early?

"Yeah. I got into the private school I applied to in Massachusetts, and it's the best one there. My parents want us to move there early so that I can get used to life and get accustomed to the workload. I'll be finishing middle school there," he says, rubbing the back of his head with his hand.

His face grows concerned when he seems to realize something.

"Wait, Sanah, this isn't because of you. Please don't think that it is. This was my top choice school, and I'm moving because of that. My parents just want me to get used to life in Massachusetts before the school stress starts."

My heart lightens a little, but it still hurts, it still hurts, it still hurts so so bad.

Cruise steps a little closer to me, reaching out to pull me close. Our faces are mere inches away from each other, and my breath hitches when his soft, gray eyes stare into mine, the storm within them gone.

"Sanah, I'll be honest, when I heard you that day, I don't think I've ever felt that sad. That really, really hurt. You were the one person I confided in about what really happened, and then you go and do the exact thing that hurt me in the first place? That *sucked*."

His face softens when he sees mine fall, and he places his hand on my face.

"That said, I've missed you so much. Seeing you at the door made my heart leap into my throat because the sight of you just makes me happy. *You* make me happy. So, of course, I'll forgive you: you're my best friend too. And a little more than that, as you can probably tell."

I let out a laugh at that, sniffling.

"I want to enjoy these last few days I have with you. I know that you mean everything you said, and I'm so glad that you're thinking this way. You deserve everything, Sunny. Don't ever let anyone make you feel otherwise."

He pulls me into a hug, tightly wrapping his arms around my waist. I wrap mine around his neck, smiling into his shoulder.

"We're good. Remember, you're my person, Sunny.

"And you're mine, Cruise."

CHAPTER SEVENTEEN

★ ★ ★

"Boo, loser," I hear Cruise's voice say as he shoves me. I yelp as I stumble forward into the hallway at school and turn back to give him a dirty look.

"This has got to be the fiftieth time I've nearly broken a bone because of your literal violence," I grumble, breaking into a grin when he wraps an arm around my shoulders.

"Ay, mind it. Annoying you is just an incomparable experience."

"Okay, you rat, that's enough. No more hugs. That's your punishment," I say, pushing him away and quickly walking forward, yelling with laughter when he pulls me back by the straps of my backpack.

"Okay, okay, sorry. Don't do that to me, please," he says as he hugs me tighter as we walk.

It's been a couple of days since my visit to Cruise, and even though this is the first time I've talked to Cruise at school since crafting that plan of mine in my bedroom a few weeks ago, it's the first time that I'm not scared about what my friends are going to say. As we walk towards the area where my group usually meets, Cruise slows his pace.

"Are you sure you don't want me to go with you? Especially with what you plan to do today."

I mull over it for a few seconds and then nod. "Yeah. It would prevent Silke from getting any points over me. I want full control today."

He nods at me and then grins wide. "Go slam 'em, my girl."

I grin back and quickly walk toward my friends, staying on the edge of the group. Today, I leave. Today, I choose myself.

"Is that Sanah that I see?" comes a voice, and the group parts to let Silke walk up to me.

She has her usual haughty grin on her face, and when she comes up to me, she slings an arm around me. It feels forced and vastly different from Cruise's kind action, and while I would usually be ecstatic, I force myself not to push her away today.

"What's the latest in the world of the jerk?" she says, grinning. "Cruise, I mean," she adds when I give her a confused look.

She awaits my answer, as does the rest of the group. Most of them expect me to jump straight back into my usual slander, but this time, I won't. I'm finished.

"Nothing. In fact, quite the opposite of what you expect. He's great."

Silke's face completely changes, and the girls around us begin to murmur as well. Silke immediately becomes hostile.

"What are you talking about?" she demands, anger flaming within her eyes.

A small crowd of students has begun to gather around us at hearing the clear anger in Silke's voice, and my own friends have joined them, staring at us as we battle each other with our eyes. I gulp slightly but then catch sight of Cruise standing a distance away from the group in front of me. He must have switched positions to watch everything. He nods vigorously and gives me a thumbs-up, and my nervousness dims. I take a deep breath and start talking again.

"Yeah. He's great. I've been talking to him for the past few months, and I've become extremely close to him. He's one of my best friends," I say confidently.

Silke's face is surprisingly devoid of emotion, and I know that when this happens, she's absolutely incensed.

"So you lied?"

"Yes," I say determinedly. "I did." I take a deep breath and look at the rest of the group. "Come on. Do you really think I could have told you guys? Look at how you reacted the first time you saw us together. You guys forced me to lie. This isn't the first time I've had to do this. You guys made me feel so uncomfortable about *everything* in general, to the point where I had to completely change myself to fit in with you guys. But it still doesn't do anything because you guys still hurt me. Remember how I left the sleepover early? I wasn't sick. I was just so hurt by the way you guys reacted to the activity I wanted to do that I left. Cruise hung out with me that day. We went to the bookstore together. It's something that you guys would never do with me, for which reason I'm *glad* I'm friends with him."

I turn to look at Silke directly now, ready to confront her with the truth. "And what are you being so hypocritical for? Didn't you lie too? When were you planning to tell us that you had manipulated us into thinking that Cruise had messed with you when you were the one who had made his life miserable? That you created those accounts on your own and trapped Cruise in your twisted narrative?"

Silke's eyes widen, and the rest of the girls freeze, realizing they've been caught. The people around us begin to murmur as they're presented with this new informemation.

"What on *earth* are you talking about? Your antics with Cruise have already established that you're a liar, but you don't need to prove it anymore," Silke says, the desperation on her face clear.

I smile slightly, pull out my phone, and open my camera roll to the screenshots Cruise sent me. The day I made up with Cruise, we decided that in order for my plan to work, we would need those pictures. Luckily, when we texted his family friend to ask for her permission to show them to her, she was totally alright with it. She was surprised Cruise didn't use the pictures earlier because she never cared what Silke thought about her and was more than happy to bring Silke's lies to light.

I hold up the screenshots to Silke. "Read, please."

Confused, she leans in, and the moment she takes in the words on the page, her face drops, and she pales, stumbling back a little.

"Where did you get this from?" she says in a hushed, gritty voice, her panic clear.

"That isn't important. What is important, though, is that this proves that you're a *liar*, that you will do anything to get your way. That stuff with Cruise was never true: it was all *you*. You couldn't keep your jealousy or anger in check, and that led to you ruining another kid's life. You let the whole school believe that Cruise was a horrible person when it's *you* that's the problem."

Whispers begin to come from the crowd, and I look around to see people with shocked looks on their faces. I can already feel the negative energy toward Cruise fading. I turn and look back at the rest of the group now, making direct eye contact with Fay and Klyah for a few seconds. The shocked, confused looks on their faces just confirm the story I narrated. Even though my heart sinks when I realize that the two people who I considered to be some of my closest friends never really cared about me, I'm glad I'll get to move on now.

I sneak a quick glance at where I last left Cruise, and he stands there with a huge smile on his face, looking immensely proud. I smile back, and when Silke turns around to look at who I'm looking at and sees Cruise, her face gets even stonier.

"I'm done trying to be someone I'm not," I say to finish. "You guys can be friends with me for who I am. Not who you want me to be."

I turn and walk away from them, passing straight by everyone's shocked glances and toward Cruise. He grins even wider at me, and when I reach him, he slings an arm around my shoulders and walks away with me into the sunlight outside the veranda.

"Well done, Sunny. Well done."

"Thanks," I say, blushing. "I wasn't that nervous, surprisingly."

"Not surprising to me. You were finally saying what you truly wanted to say. It must have felt great," he says, shrugging.

"It did."

I stop walking and pull Cruise to face me. Surprised, he stares down at me, and I smile.

"Thank you, Cruise. Thank you so much for showing me what I could have never realized on my own. Thank you for everything."

He smiles softly, leans in, and gives me a quick kiss on the cheek. My face turns red, and Cruise laughs.

"Of course, Sunny. I'm always going to be there for you. No matter where I am."

He hugs me, and we stay like that for a few moments, ignoring the surprised looks and whispers of the people around us, all of whom have been inundated with new gossip. I take in as much of him as I can, savoring some of the last few moments I have with him. While I'll miss him more than words can express, I'm beyond grateful for him. And I'm not scared of being alone anymore because there's nothing wrong with it. There's no point in surrounding myself with people who don't care about me. I'd rather be more content on my own. Besides, I know I won't *really* be lonely. I have Cruise—my one *true* friend—my family, and myself.

And that is more than enough for me to be happy.

EPILOGUE

★   ★   ★

The final school bell rings sharply, and the sounds of the bustle of students and scrapes of chairs fill the air around me. I pack up my stuff, too, getting up and pushing my chair in as I do. I sling my backpack over my shoulder and wait for the crowd around the door to my classroom to dissipate and exit after it does. The weather and beams of the sun match that of the day Cruise and I first started talking, and I smile softly when I think of him. I pull out my phone, shooting him a quick "I miss you" text, and he responds with a heart a few seconds after. My smile gets a little bigger, and it remains on my face as I tuck my phone away and start toward the exit of the school. I turn into the long hallway that leads to the side door I usually take to walk home, groups of students clustered on either side. As I walk, I spot my old friend group standing on the right, and I falter, my steps slowing. A small bloom of fury and despair grows within me when I see them chatting excitedly with each other. I would be lying if I said the last few weeks hadn't been weird. After spending so long with a group of people, losing them takes a while to get used to. However, while I do feel upset, I feel no inclination to join them, no regret. I only miss the company they provided. I don't miss *them*. And it is that proud realization that pushes me to walk confidently past them, staring straight ahead as I feel their resentful eyes on me. I'm alright with being on my own if it means I don't surround myself with those who don't care about me or my happiness. As I walk down the hallway alone, surrounded by other excited groups of friends walking together or standing still to talk, I'm at peace with my loneliness.

I'm alone, but not lonely.

And that is quite alright with me.

ACKNOWLEDGMENTS

I've been very lucky to be surrounded by a group of incredible people while I wrote this book. I couldn't ask for better company.

To my mentor and editor, Beth Spencewood: thank you for helping me make a childhood dream of mine come true. It has been a true pleasure working with you.

To my incredible *mama* and *papa*: thank you for your endless support. This wouldn't have been possible without you guys. I know you'll be frowning in the morning when I tell you that I wrote this dedication at 4 A.M., but I love y'all. Thank you for being my biggest motivators and my best friends in the whole world: I owe you guys everything.

To my lovely sister: thank you for cheering from the sidelines. Your belief in me never wavers no matter what happens, and I'm so grateful for you.

To my *chacha, masi,* Siya, and Arjun: thank you for always being there for me. I promise I'll come out of my room more.

To my grandparents: thank you for your prayers and your never-ending comfort.

To my books: thank you for being my inspiration and my friends when I had no one else.

To all the friends I lost along the way: thank you for helping me grow. I miss you guys every day, but sometimes, we're forced to close a chapter we never wanted to end in order to learn from it.

And to my current, boisterous, crazy group: thank you for making all those years of loneliness worth it.

AUTHOR BIOGRAPHY

★ ★ ★

Tvisha Gupta is a senior who fell in love with reading and literature during her childhood in India. She's someone who always has her nose buried in a book, and her favorite book genres are thriller and fantasy. When she isn't writing creative short stories or journalistic articles, Tvisha can be found playing the piano, drinking an unhealthy amount of coffee as she watches Gilmore Girls in her bed, or going for long-distance runs during the sunset. In the future, Tvisha hopes to be a journalist or an editor for a literary magazine.